She moved! ... rcus almost
hurled him ... firm hold of
his fear. Sh ... earth could
break free from a bellspell. It was only his imagination,
or maybe a small shaking of the web as he set the fly.
That would be it right enough: a shaking of the web.

He was reaching for a third fly when the spinner's
foreleg flickered out towards him. The viciously
hooked claw sliced through his gauntlet as if it were
paper, then ripped along his arm and embedded briefly
in his shoulder.

With a howl of terror, Marcus flung himself away.
He lost his kneehold on the web at once and fell
between the strands. He grabbed and missed. His
pail toppled, fell, spilling agitated blue flies into the
yawning pit below. He watched them tumble, tumble,
slow as thistledown. Then his body arched out after
them.

He could hear a scream and knew it was his own.

MARCUS MUSTARD

J. H. BRENNAN

BANTAM BOOKS

TORONTO · NEW YORK · LONDON · SYDNEY · AUCKLAND

MARCUS MUSTARD

A BANTAM BOOK : 0 553 40705 8

First publication in Great Britain

PRINTING HISTORY
Bantam edition published 1994

Set in Linotype Palatino 11/12pt by
Hewer Text Composition Services, Edinburgh

Bantam Books are published by Transworld Publishers Ltd,
61–63 Uxbridge Road, Ealing, London W5 5SA,
in Australia by Transworld Publishers (Australia) Pty Ltd,
15–25 Helles Avenue, Moorebank, NSW 2170,
and in New Zealand by Transworld Publishers (NZ) Ltd,
3 William Pickering Drive, Albany, Auckland.

Printed and bound in Great Britain by
Cox & Wyman Ltd, Reading, Berks.

For Jim,
whose creative mind supplied the ending.
With love and thanks.

Chapter One

The huge, flightless bluebottles, each one larger than a tomcat, crawled slowly over rotting offal in the bottom of the trough. Their wings vibrated busily, but were too short to lift them. *Live food*, Marcus Mustard thought as he looked at them. It was the first thing they taught a 'prentice: the spinners only eat live food.

He was holding his breath because of the smell and it was beginning to burn his lungs. He reached in quickly and caught one of the giant insects. It buzzed angrily as he dropped it into the pail and reached for another. The rushlight reflected on the creature's scaling, causing an effect like oil on water.

The moment his pail was full (and heavy) he moved from the troughs and released his breath explosively. He had enough to feed four spinners before having to come back for more. So it would go through the morning, perhaps through the whole day if he couldn't change duty following the noon salute. It wasn't so bad, provided he remembered to hold his breath. The bluebottles stank – a harsh, metallic insect smell – but not half so bad as the offal.

His pail buzzed and hummed as he carried it towards the spinner caverns. These were guarded like the apprentice cellar where he lived and slept. But the cellar had only one old soldier to look after it: the caverns had real guards, broad-shouldered, hard-muscled, cold-eyed, with swords so fine-edged they could split a hair. They were at the entrances day and night, wary to the point of murderous with strangers. Castle Dis lived on silk, and Lord Leon Dark wanted none of its secrets carried to the outside world.

Marcus nodded at the guards and walked past without causing much more than a flicker of an eye. But this was only because he was known. On his first day he had been stopped and searched and questioned until tears of terror and frustration streamed down his cheeks. Aye, and on the second and third day too; and on all the days of the second and third week. But they got to know him eventually.

He entered the caverns and stepped on to the catwalk that ran around the galleries. This had once frightened him even more than the guards. Below him was a drop so immense as to appear bottomless. (And Bracket, who took pleasure in the fear of others, claimed it really *was* bottomless.) Above him, the roof of the caverns soared like some great cathedral. And all around, the granite archways, pavements, tunnels, galleries and cliff-faces that made the caverns such a perfect home for spinners.

The catwalk, like the ladders which reached out from it, was of wood, part jointed but mainly lashed with cable silk so that it creaked and swayed endlessly. It was secure enough – cable silk would easily outlast the wood – but hardly safe, for there were no sides and only a single cable strand as hand-rail. If a boy lost his footing, he would tumble and fall. Even if Bracket were wrong, he must die when he hit the bottom. It had happened; and when it happened, there was not even an attempt at rescue, so certain were the masters that to fall was death.

Marcus pushed the grim thoughts from his head, for all knew that grim thoughts called ill luck. His step was confident enough, if slow, like a Bishop's tread, and he swung his buzzing pail to compensate for the movement of the catwalk. There were glowglobes here – nothing was too good for the spinners – but set low because the creatures disliked bright light and would not produce well in it. Nevertheless, he spotted the new web easily enough and climbed the nearest ladder.

Marcus was a sturdy boy, but even so the pail was beginning to hurt his arm by the time he reached the web. He could already see the spinner, a dark shape about the size of a bull mastiff crouched high above in the shelter of a granite arch. She had seen him too, he was certain. He could imagine the horseshoe of black eyes watching his every move. He could imagine the hunger in her and the ferocity and excitement.

Her position was such that she could drop directly on him, but he knew she would not. He was safe enough provided he did not shake the web. Moving with enormous care now (this was the point, the Masters said, at which a 'prentice was most likely to be killed), he shifted the pail from his right hand to his left and fished in the pocket of his jerkin for the little spellbell. All the time he watched her, despite the claims that a spinner would not move if he didn't touch her web. None ever had, but he saw no sense in lowering his guard.

His hand closed on the spellbell, cool from the magic it contained, and he drew it out. His movements were very deliberate. The problem was that the ladder itself was drawn close, so if it shifted too much, it might touch the web and trigger a response. Should she launch herself upon him, he was dead for sure. The ferocity of the spinners was legendary and they carried poison in their fangs. He thought now, as he had often thought before, that if she dropped, he would step from the ladder. Better to die cleanly in a fall than lie paralysed, half-conscious, while the spinner fed on him.

She shifted her position and his heart lurched in terrified response, but she did not drop and now he had the bell free. Relief flooded through him as he rang it firmly.

The spinner twitched once, then froze into immobility as the magic reached her on the sweet, clear chime. Marcus put the bell away and climbed on to the web. He was in no hurry. This too had been drummed into him. The spell would last no less than half an hour – time enough and plenty to do what he had to do. He kept knees and elbows firmly on the long vertical strands which were free of glue – the same ones the spinner used to scuttle down the web in search of prey. So long as he avoided the cross-strands, he was safe. The web looked flimsy, but spinner silk was stronger than any other thing in the whole Alizarin creation. He could not break through it if he tried.

Moving with that ungainly, deliberate gait all 'prentices developed for their web-work, he crawled towards the immobile spinner. She was an ugly brute close up: eight hairy legs, a bloated body, eight eyes ringed around a fanged head. Had he been walking upright, she would have stood at least waist high. As it was, she seemed to loom over him while he crawled the web on all fours. Although he had made this crawl a thousand times before, he still shuddered as he reached her. In the lower levels, worked only by the Masters, they said there were spinners larger than dray horses, producing cable thick as a man's wrist. Marcus hoped he never lived to see one. The dog-sized spinners on the upper levels were frightening enough.

He hung the pail on the web itself – the hook was impregnated with a magical smoke-oil which ensured it would not stick – and sat back on his heels. For some reason he felt compelled to watch the spinner as he reached for the first fat fly. He knew she couldn't move, but there was nothing to indicate her restraints – no glow, no shimmering in the air to show that magic touched her. She crouched so close he could easily have reached out and stroked the tuft of hair above the nearest claw. He could actually see his own image reflected in the liquid surface of her frontmost eyes. Nothing stood between them, nothing protected him except that single note of magic.

Marcus pushed that grim thought aside as well and placed the struggling bluebottle on a cross-strand of the web. It stuck at once and though it jerked and fought to get away, it stuck firm. Was there a change in the spinner's eyes, despite the stasis that held her? Did her hunger increase with the prey so close?

He thought he saw her eyes flicker. Marcus blinked. The eyes could not possibly flicker. The bellspell held everything in stasis – everything. It was in the nature of the magic that the creature became absolutely immobile, locked in an instant of time that would not move on until the spell wore off. He shook his head and smiled a little at his foolishness. The spinner's eyes could not have moved. He lifted out another bluebottle and placed it on the web.

She moved! He was certain she moved. Marcus almost hurled himself backwards before he caught firm hold of his fear. She had not moved. No spinner on earth could break free from a bellspell. It was only his imagination, or maybe a small shaking of the web as he set the fly. That would be it right enough: a shaking of the web.

He was reaching for a third fly when the spinner's foreleg flickered out towards him. The viciously hooked claw sliced through his gauntlet as if it were paper, then ripped along his arm and embedded briefly in his shoulder.

With a howl of terror, Marcus flung himself away. He lost his kneehold on the web at once and fell between the strands. He grabbed and missed. His pail toppled, fell, spilling agitated blue flies into the yawning pit below. He watched them tumble, tumble, slow as thistledown. Then his body arched out after them.

He could hear a scream and knew it was his own.

Chapter Two

There had been omens of Marcus Mustard's death in the strange start to the day. For the third time that week, Marcus had awakened to the sound of singing.

Everything else was as it should have been. He lay beneath his hides in the cellar, warmed by the body-heat of his fellow apprentices. On his right, Mo-Mo-Molestrangler, sleeping like the dead. On his left, Cloydd, the little white-haired, pink-eyed hunchback who shook and shivered with each breath. Beyond his head, sprawled crosswise, the odious Bracket. Beyond his feet, the cheerful Prunebane, who claimed to be the son of Bishop Puddifat. And beyond them the others, like a ragged sea that generated gasps and snorts and snores and sometimes ruder noises accompanied by smells.

Near the curtained archway he could see Blockstump, their guard, dozing half propped on his useless pike. Blockstump was missing nearly all his left leg. A worn leather apron served as armour and when his eyes flickered open in the soft glow of the night-light, it was obvious that one of them was blind. Molestrangler swore his sword was rusted in its scabbard.

Marcus could feel the lumbering vibration of the great pumps circulating air into the silk pits, but this was a background noise he would never really notice unless it stopped. His mind, his whole attention, was swallowed by the singing.

It had the sound of women's voices, pitched high, pure and clear. Though he could not quite make out the words, the melody was plaintive. It carried his thoughts sweeping upwards along the labyrinthine levels of Castle Dis until they emerged to soar through cumulus and sunlight, wheeling and turning like a bird in flight.

The sound seemed entirely real, as if a soprano choir had crept into the cellar. But he knew it was not real and would fade. As it did. In a moment, the melody existed only in his mind, sinuously curling in and out of his thoughts.

Prunebane and Molestrangler were both convinced the singing was some sort of sign, or omen, sent to Marcus only. Bracket, who was jealous of the attention, claimed darkly that it was a portent of death, probably Marcus's own, and now it looked as though he might be right.

Marcus had crept slowly out from under the hides as the singing faded. For warmth, he slept in shirt and breeches, so he had only to pull on the tattered jerkin and his pointed shoes. He moved quietly. The other 'prentices were still asleep, but would not be for long and first up got the best cheese.

Marcus climbed over the prostrate bodies with great care. Any he woke, with the possible exception of Cloydd, who was sickly, would catch his ankle and try to throw him down so they could reach the kitchen first. Morning was always a rough and tumble among the 'prentices. Today, woken early by the singing, Marcus might avoid the worst of it. He enjoyed a peaceful start almost as much as he enjoyed the irritation of his friends when they tumbled into the kitchen and found him already munching.

Blockstump's good eye flickered open as Marcus passed, so perhaps he wasn't such a useless guard after all. Marcus placed a finger to his lips and Blockstump nodded conspiratorially. He was a simple soul – there was talk that some of his brain had been hacked out in the fight that cost him his leg. He seemed to like the way Marcus sneaked early to the kitchens.

Marcus slid through the curtain into the short stretch of rush-lit corridor. No daylight penetrated into the cellar or its adjoining kitchens – or anywhere at all in the silk labyrinth, come to that. The 'prentices did not warrant the luxury of glowglobes, so there were rushlights everywhere here, smoking, smelling and producing a dim, flickering light.

He must have wakened even earlier than he thought, for there was only a handful of kitchen maids about. Marcus took his familiar seat at the end of the third table and one of them limped across. 'First again, 'Prentice Marcus,' she said, grinning a snaggle-toothed grin. 'Soft cheese.'

Which was the point, of course. There was never enough soft cheese to go round, so those who came late had to make do with the hard, crumbly, stinky cheese made from mushroom milk. Those very late had to make do with rinds.

'Soft cheese,' Marcus echoed, grinning back. She was a plain girl, but he liked her for her wit. Her name was Prudence Rainwater. The limp was not an injury. It came from the fact that she was missing ties on one of her shoes and had to drag her foot to keep it on. Once Prunebane, in merry mood, had proposed marriage to her – possibly quite seriously, for Lord Dark ruled that a boy might marry at thirteen. 'Nay,' Prudence said, 'for then should I be called Pru Prune and men would say I stuttered worse than Raymond Molestrangler.'

She laid a square of hard black bread on the tabletop to serve him as a platter, then set down his battered tankard and filled it from the jug she carried. Marcus sipped the bitter ale as she limped away from the steaming pot of smoked-eel stew. She ladled a generous helping directly on to the bread, then fished a muslin-wrapped block from her apron and set it on the table with another grin. 'Soft cheese,' she said again.

'I thank thee, Mistress Prudence,' Marcus said formally. To his surprise, she flushed a little as she turned away.

The smell of the stew started his stomach grumbling and he set to. He was almost halfway through it when the roiling stampede of his fellow-apprentices finally burst through the door and began to spread among the tables like a tumbling tide. His hand went out instinctively to drop the little block of soft cheese into his pocket.

Raymond Molestrangler slid on to the bench beside him. 'P-p-players from the North Tower coming to the square today,' he said without preliminary. He was a boy who always seemed to hear things first and Marcus did not trouble to ask him how he knew.

'Today?' Marcus asked instead. 'What time they coming then?'

'After Lauds,' Molestrangler told him. 'To s-s-s-celebrate the ngeh-Refreshing.' He had a husky voice that managed to make his stammer sound even worse.

Marcus wrinkled his nose. Lauds was three of

16

the clock for those who bothered. 'I be on double shift today.' It was a pity. Players were a rare enough entertainment, even local players. But players from the North Tower were a real novelty. The North Tower was two days' march along the convoluted streets and corridors of Castle Dis.

'And they b-b-be here tomorrow and the next day,' Molestrangler smiled knowingly. 'Freshing b-b-bain't till Thorsday.'

'Then I go tomorrow,' Marcus told him, pleased. He wondered if he should ask Prudence to come with him. She was born somewhere near the North Tower. He looked round, but the kitchens were full now and in the crush and the noise he could no longer see her.

The noise died a little when the Masters arrived: Starkk, Morrigam and Trisram today, not the worst of them. Morrigam chose Marcus's table. He was a square, muscular man with a bald, bullet head and nervous eyes, but even-tempered enough if people did their work. He drank the token mug of ale slowly, so that the other tables were cleared before Marcus received his first assignment. Not that he was in any hurry. As he had gloomily suspected, he was on a feeding detail.

Prunebane, who had been instructed to do baling, said cheerfully, 'At least it's not cleaning.'

'A blessing,' Marcus said. Feeding was bad, but cleaning, the thorough weekly cleaning that carted off the wastes as well as washing out the troughs, was definitely worse. But then, apart from feeding and cleaning, there was only watching, which was a bore, baling, which was a bore, and stacking, which was back-breaking. When you thought on it, there was not much pleasure in the work at all.

Come the day, though, when 'prenticeship was over and he became a Master. Then he could live out of the pits and marry on to a woman skilled at the pot. And tell others what to do.

He and Prunebane left the kitchens together, nudging one another boisterously. But since Prunebane had to bale, he turned towards the storage sheds. Marcus collected his pail and his gauntlets then walked alone to the feeding troughs and his grim destiny.

Chapter Three

The jolt was so sharp, so sudden that he felt his shoulder dislocate. Somehow the pain was less than it should have been, as if it was presented to him wrapped in cloth.

He had stopped falling. He felt strange.

Marcus was sure he had stopped falling, although his mind was confused. After the jolt he had begun to twist so that the galleries, archways and catwalk whirled past in a bewildering blur. As he twisted, he swung in a huge, mind-numbing arc, to and fro, to and fro . . .

Under the wrapped pain of the dislocation, there was a knot of fire in his shoulder. There was a river of pain along the whole of his right arm. There was wool in his head, so his thoughts grew soft and blurred.

To and fro . . .

Peacefully, painfully, to and fro . . .

The world passed away, then returned. He felt as if he had slept, but if he slept, there was no singing. He felt ill, or at least not well, or at least not normal. He felt dead. Perhaps he *was* dead. Once he had heard a priest say that some people survived death, even if they did not have the money for the magic. It was hard to believe.

Marcus, perhaps dead, tried to hum to himself in time with the swinging pendulum. To and fro . . . to and fro . . .

He looked down and his heart chilled. He was swinging over the abyss of the silk pits.

With a huge effort he turned his head. He looked upwards and felt such terror that he almost fainted. He was swinging on a single silken thread. The spinner had attached it to his shoulder when she mounted her attack. Now he looked up along it and his stomach heaved in fear. At one end of the thread swung Marcus. At the other, crouched the spinner in her web.

Marcus turned again and vomited into the abyss. He experienced a horror that clung to every fibre of his body. He wished he were cleanly dead, crushed by the fall, at the bottom of the silk pits. He wished he did not know what would happen to him now.

But he did know. He was trapped. The spinner had attached a cable to him, piercing his skin and fusing her silk to the shoulder-bone beneath. It was what spinners did with prey that avoided the web but came too close. Now he swung at the end of the silk and soon the spinner would begin to reel him in. He was almost twice her body-weight, but spinners were strong and patient as the grave. If it took her a day to reel him in, she would have him.

When she had him, she would feed. *Live food*, he thought and came close to vomiting again.

Could he escape? Not with his life, for sure, but he might escape spinner death, which was the worst of deaths. Spinner silk would not be broken and to free the fusion from the bone did not bear thinking of. But silk could be cut and Marcus had his 'prentice knife.

He required to move fast, for soon he would not move at all. Spinners liked live food, but did not care to eat a struggling prey. They injected poison at the moment of attack. The prey did not die, but lost the power to move. In that state it was eaten.

This was why his dislocated shoulder was giving him so little pain. The venom had gone in with the silk and was spreading as he swung. Already his movements were sluggish. In a while they would stop. Then he would feel no pain at all, nor would he move. He would see, he would hear, he would think. He would watch her reel him in and watch her feast until he died. But he would not struggle.

With his right arm almost useless, Marcus used his left to fish for the knife in his jacket pocket. His fingers closed on an object and he pulled it out. Not the knife, but the wrap of soft cheese – with something written on the muslin which, in the gloom, he could not read. Soft cheese. He would never eat it. For an instant he thought to drop it, then stupidly slid it back into his pocket. Soft cheese was hard won. What matter that he would soon plunge to his death; this cheese was his.

He found the knife with its string-wrapped handle, drew it out and dropped it. Marcus watched it tumble into darkness, his mind numb. How could he? How could he have dropped his single chance?

The arcs of his pendulum grew shorter. His twisting had already slowed. Soon all motion stopped and he hung from one hunched, dead shoulder over the abyss. He could feel the chill paralysis creeping through his limbs.

His head felt so large he could scarce move it. But move it he did, to look along the silk line. The spinner was still crouched as she had been from the very start. In fact, now he thought on it, her only movement had been that single, savage lashing of the claw. Did the spell still hold? Had the magic worked in part?

Marcus frowned slowly. His thoughts swam through his head like giant turtles. He knew little of wizards' business, but he had never known a bellspell to fail, never even heard talk of failure. Sometimes the bell ran out of magic and felt warm and would not chime, but that was a different thing. If it was present, magic always worked. The bellspells made to hold the spinners were well-designed. They had been used in the silk pits of Castle Dis for centuries.

The numbness spread from his shoulder throughout his body and he did not care. It reached his legs, which now felt heavy as they dangled over the abyss. A strange calm descended on him. He raised his eyes and looked up to the spinner at the far end of the thread. She still had not moved. But she must move soon. Even if the spell had worked to full effect, it would crumble after thirty minutes at the most.

As his body stilled, Marcus found his senses sharpened. At this distance, he could smell the spinner; separate her body-scent from the glue-smell of the web. There was none of the metallic edge that clung to the bluebottles. Spinner scent was sweet, like an exotic flower. His eyes functioned better as well. Even in the dim light, he could make out the subtle banding of her fur. His hearing grew more acute. He could hear mice scuttling on their trackways in the cliff-face. He could hear the creak of the catwalk.

He could hear voices! They were distant, but he could hear them.

Help me! Marcus screamed. But the scream did not reach his lips, for there was no function in

22

his throat. He hung over the abyss and gradually the voices faded away. Marcus wept until his eyes locked so that he could no longer weep. He hung, immobile. He could see only a portion of a granite arch and the gloom beyond. He could no longer look up to see the spinner.

Help me, Marcus whimpered in his mind.

Marcus wished to close his eyes, but could not. There was only the arch and the gloom.

The voices came again, nearer this time. But he could not understand them. He heard the words clearly, yet they carried no meaning. That would be the action of the venom on his brain, he thought sluggishly. He could see, hear, smell, taste, but could not move and could extract too little meaning from the world around him.

Time . . . how much time had passed? How soon would the spinner waken?

He felt a tug on the silk strand and fear washed away his unnatural calm. The spinner had begun to reel him in!

Inside his mind, Marcus howled with terror. He screamed, struck out, fought, kicked and bit. But his body remained motionless, suspended from one hunched shoulder by a single strand of silk.

He did not appear to be moving, but the strand was vibrating lightly. He remembered. He had watched spinners reeling in their prey. Before they began, they touched the strand again and again, felt it, fondled it, delicately stroked it. Why, he did not know. But it was happening now, he was certain. The spinner was awake – was preparing to draw him in.

The tremors travelling down the strand grew gross. He even began to turn around again, slowly, so that his eyes travelled away from the arch to take in a tunnel entrance, then the empty catwalk, then ridging in the granite cliff-face, then, slowly, the arch again and onwards. What was shaking the silk strand so much?

He hung, shoulder raised, and felt sweat trickle from his forehead into his open eyes, blurring even his restricted vision. Fear rose to such a pitch that it cleared his thoughts. The spinner was moving now all right. She was climbing down the strand.

He had seen this too before, though rarely. Rather than reel up, the spinner would sometimes fix the strand then spin another and lower herself on that. As she went, she gripped the first strand as a guideline, drew the two together and feasted when she reached her prey. Perhaps it was done when the prey was heavy, as he would be heavy to a spinner of her size. He did not know. He only knew it was done. He only knew the spinner was coming for him down the thread.

The shaking of the strand grew more pronounced. With his venom-sharpened senses, Marcus could actually feel her body-heat as she approached, although the flower-scent was not so strong as he would have expected; not strong at all, in fact, and overlaid by something else, like musty cheese.

There would be a probing first. The spinners were cautious. One clawed foreleg would reach out with a feather touch and shake the prey as a man might shake a sleeping friend to wake him. If the prey remained still, the spinner fed.

He felt a light touch on his shoulder. If he could move now, even a little, the spinner would back away. Marcus focused his will. He must move. His life depended on it. But he could not move.

Suddenly his shoulder erupted in a flowering of the most intense pain he had ever known. It broke through the venom-numbness to send a flare of agony across the muscling of his upper body. Again he tried to scream, again could not. It felt as though the spinner had reached inside him to touch the very bone. It felt as if the spinner had begun to feed.

A voice, shouting. And so close it might have been inches from his ear. Did the spinner withdraw a little? Certainly the agony in his shoulder lessened, although it did not go completely.

There was a new vibration on the strand, then suddenly, smoothly, he was moving upwards. Yet the spinner was still on the strand. He could sense her crouching just above him and a little to the rear. What was happening? He stopped for a heartbeat, then moved smoothly up again. For the third time he began, slowly, to twist. He saw her then, a hunched dark shape. As he turned, he saw her eyes, smaller than he remembered and no longer black, but glowing a brilliant yellow. Then, still turning, he went beyond her and moved upwards, smooth as smoke, until he reached the web.

Hands caught him. Not spinner claws, but hands. The familiar touch brought flooding relief and his mind cleared. When the voices came, he recognized them, understood them. Prunebane and Molestrangler were gripping him. Even Bracket was there. Behind them, standing easily upright, was Master Starkk, a man so long-limbed he looked a little like a spinner himself.

The thing behind him on the strand jumped and scampered off across the web. No spinner this, but Cloydd the albino cruikback with his wetly hanging lip and pink-red eyes. He turned, looked back and grinned.

'Brave boy,' Master Starkk commended him.

'Get him netted. We bain't got much time!' It was Master Morrigam's voice, somewhere below.

'That we bain't,' Starkk agreed. 'Nor would I stay here longer nor I have to, Strang. Leastwise, not until I know what happened here.'

They wrapped Marcus in thick netting for carrying. It was not spinner silk, but strong enough. Molestrangler and Prunebane gripped an end. Bracket reached out to steady. 'Lower him easy, lads,' Strang Morrigam commanded from below. As they began to lower him, the angle of his vision changed and he saw the spinner still crouched beneath her archway.

He was bouncing against the ladder, then Morrigam's broad hands gripped him. He had a fleeting glimpse of naked scabrous scalp before his face was pressed into the back of Morrigam's rough jacket. The catwalk creaked and swayed as he was carried out.

Running footsteps, then the hoarse voice of a guard. 'What happened here?'

'Spinner got him,' Morrigam said shortly.

'Be he dead?' A bearded face swam into Marcus's field of vision and swung towards him until he was aware only of one enormous peering eye.

'Good as,' sniffed Morrigam and the face withdrew.

His head bumped rhythmically against Morrigam's hard back as he was carried to the 'prentice cellar. 'That be young Mustard!' he heard in the familiar sing-song of Blockstump's voice, then the curious *clunk-thud* of his carved-wood

26

leg as he hurried after them. 'What happened, Master Morrigam? What happened?'

'Spinner,' Morrigam explained again.

'Mother Goddess and Her Holy Twins!' Blockstump exclaimed. Marcus could imagine him making the Sign of Horns.

He was laid almost tenderly on a pile of skins. As he rolled on to his back, he could see the faces of his friends ranged all around him and the faces of Masters Morrigam and Starkk. The men looked grim, but the boys just looked frightened. He wished he could speak, to tell them it was all right now; he would not be eaten by a spinner.

'What's the matter with him, Master?' Prunebane asked.

'Poison, boy,' Starkk said.

'Spinner must have bit him,' Morrigam grunted.

Not a bite, Marcus thought. *She hooked me with her claw.* But he couldn't speak to tell them.

'How could she, Master?' Prunebane's voice again.

Morrigam sniffed. 'Happen he forgot to ring his spellbell, silly little scrog.'

I didn't forget! Marcus screamed. *I didn't forget!* No sound emerged.

'Will he d-d-die?' Molestrangler asked.

'Aye,' said Morrigam, 'and soon, lessen we get help for him. Spinner poison stops yer moving, like he be now. But then it softens yer insides to jelly so she can suck them out. That happens, you're dead. Not even magic can turn that.'

'But we can get magic to turn the poison,' the lisping voice of cruikback Cloydd put in. 'There's magic for that, Master, sure enough.'

'Sure enough,' Master Starkk's voice echoed. 'But where would a 'prentice find the gold to buy it?'

27

'Or a Master neither,' grunted Morrigam sourly.

'We'll g-give what we can,' Molestrangler said. 'I have two p-p-p-pennies I was saving to see the p-p-p-players. He can have that.'

Morrigam's voice softened. 'You're a good lad, Raymond, but think on this, boy: it takes twelve of your copper pennies to make one piece of silver and twenty silver pieces to make one piece of gold. There's not a wizard in the whole of Dis would make you magic to turn poison for less than fifteen gold, Goddess curse them and their greed. So where's your two pennies now?'

There was silence in the cellar. Staring upwards out of eyes he could not close, Marcus wondered how long it would take before his insides turned to jelly.

'Sir,' Prunebane said urgently, 'we must do something! I can give a penny too.'

'Best leave him to die,' Morrigam said gently. 'At least he'll feel no pain.'

But Starkk said, 'We might try taking him to Squat. He's glad of pennies now.'

'Erasmus Squat? That old quack?' Morrigam exclaimed.

Marcus's head rolled to one side and as it did so, he glimpsed Starkk shrug. 'He's dead if he lies here,' Starkk said. 'Better for us all that he should die with Squat.'

'That's true enough,' said Morrigam at once.

Chapter Four

The sunlight stung his eyes, but he could not close them. They put him in a dog-cart and covered him with a tattered blanket. All the 'prentices wanted to come, but Strang Morrigam sent them packing. Life or death, there was still work to do. Then he whipped up the pit-bull and trotted behind as Marcus bounced loose-limbed along the cobbled roadway.

The streets of Castle Dis were packed as ever, swollen both by the stream of traders who had business at the silk pits and by Outland pilgrims gathered to experience the Refreshing due in two days. The traders wore colourful garments and often carried pennants. The pilgrims, in the main, were dour, especially the followers of Wormwood.

The crowds scarcely thinned when they reached Reditch, the district where Master Squat plied his illegal trade, but they certainly grew more disreputable. Here the streets became a warren, overhung by houses which seemed to have a beggar in every doorway. Corner louts watched passers-by with predatory interest, but nobody bothered Morrigam, who was broad-shouldered and looked dangerous. His spinner insignia, marking him as a wrangler, was enough to make sure no-one thought him rich.

The apothecary shop was in the basement of a grubby building that stank of cabbage. Strang Morrigam tethered the cart to the railings and set the dog to guard it. Then he carried Marcus, well wrapped in the blanket, down the worn stone steps.

With his heightened perceptions, Marcus felt his head reel when the smells first hit him. The shop was low-ceilinged, gloomy and empty of customers, but not of stock. Sacks, trays, boxes, jars and cabinets took up almost every available square inch of space and more of its wares, including several desiccated lizards, hung from the beams. Strang cleared a swathe of counter space with a sweep of his arm and laid Marcus upon it. He looked around impatiently, then found a brass handbell and rang it.

'My dear sir, profoundly sorry to have kept you waiting!' The man who emerged from the back room was thin as a victim of the plague, with both the nose and the breath of one who drank sembala spirit. He wore the robes and skullcap of a scholar.

'Be thee Master Squat the doctor?' Strang asked.

'Erasmus Squat, sir, at your service, but doctor no longer, I fear – at least, in the eyes of the authorities who frown on the foibles of suffering humanity. But that is not to say you may not find a cure here, for have I not the finest tincture of unicorn, the most potent of mummy dust, the most sovereign—'

Strang drew back the blanket. 'This 'prentice,' he broke in. 'He be poisoned.'

Squat leaned across to stare into Marcus Mustard's open eyes. 'What happened?'

'Spinner got him.'

'How long ago?' Squat asked.

'An hour since.' Strang shrugged. 'Maybe more.'

'He'll be dead soon,' Squat said.

'Less you do something on it.'

Squat looked up at him soberly. 'I, sir? Had you not heard I have been forbidden medical practice?'

'I'd heard.' He fished in his jacket and placed a small purse on the counter next to Marcus's head.

Squat glanced at the purse, then back at Morrigam. The tip of his tongue flicked out to lick his lips. It was a nervous gesture that made him look like one of his own desiccated lizards. 'You know what Lord Dark's people do to you for practising medicine when you've been barred?'

'Jail you,' Strang said shortly.

Squat shook his head. 'They remove the smallest digit of each hand. The next time you are caught, it's the thumbs. After that, you lose your hands completely.'

Strang looked down at Marcus. 'Name of Mustard. Thirteen, fourteen years of age – I'm not rightly sure, but he be one good 'prentice. Bain't no way he deserves this.' He looked up at Squat. 'Spinner poison liquefies your guts. He's dying, Master Squat. Said so yourself.'

There was a long, silent moment, then Squat picked up the purse. 'Bring him in the back.'

The back room was even darker than the store – so gloomy that there was a lighted oil lamp on the table. The room was just as cluttered as the store, except that here the clutter was mainly books – heavy, leather-bound tomes of great age.

'Lay him there,' Squat said, pushing an enormous tomcat off a sagging couch. As Master

Morrigam laid Marcus down, his staring eyes slid over an open cabinet of surgeon's tools.

'How much is in the purse?' asked Squat bluntly. He shook it in his hand so the coins jingled.

'Three silver,' Strang said. It was in copper coin to make the purse seem fatter.

'My fee is five,' Squat said. He had delicate features except for the veining of his nose.

Strang Morrigam sniffed. 'Bain't got five. Boy's a 'prentice. Copper a week and his keep.'

'Four!' bargained Squat.

'Bain't got four neither.' He nodded to the purse in Squat's hand. 'That's a collection. Pence from the lads and Masters. No more where that come from.'

They were haggling while the spinner poison worked on his insides. Marcus wanted to scream at them to hurry, but could not.

'Oh, very well!' Squat gave in gracelessly. 'But no promises. If he dies, there's no refund, you understand. And I want none of your hard men coming round at night to threaten me.'

'Wranglers threaten no man,' Morrigam said.

'Not what I heard,' Erasmus Squat said sourly. He crossed to the surgeon's cabinet and stared into it. 'Keep watch in the shop,' he ordered Morrigam.

But Morrigam was shaking his head. 'Not me, Master Squat. The boy's to be left with thee. If you get him cured, you tell him to walk back to the silk pits and sharpish.' He moved briskly to the door.

'But what if he dies?' Squat called after him.

'Then bury him!' growled Morrigam and disappeared.

'Charming!' Squat murmured half to himself. He looked over at the prostrate Marcus. 'Charming, isn't he, your friend? So polite. Well now . . .'

To Marcus's horror, he opened the leather purse and proceeded to count the coinage. Already the innards of Marcus's tight, lean body were beginning to feel peculiar. There was no pain yet, but he had the impression of things slowly softening. Desperately he tried to urge this ghastly man to hurry, but for all his efforts he could not persuade his tongue to twitch.

'. . . thirty-four . . . thirty-five . . . thirty-six!' Squat murmured. He looked over to Marcus again. 'At least he's honest. It's all here: thirty-six copper likenesses of Leon Dark, our beloved Alizarin Emperor. Well, twenty-four, to be exact. There's a dozen of the old dowager, Goddess rot her corpse. But all good coin of Dis and worth three silver as he said.' He dropped the purse into his pocket and sucked his teeth. 'But what shall we do with you?'

Marcus knew with certainty that this man in the scholar's skullcap was going to let him die. He had the money and Master Morrigam was gone. All Squat had to do was wait a while. The spinner poison would do the rest. Then, when Marcus died, Squat could bury him and keep the fee. There was no-one to swear vengeance for a 'prentice. Strang Morrigam had made it plain that even the Master Wranglers did not care.

Squat walked over to look down into Marcus's face. He rolled back his upper lip to lick his top teeth thoughtfully. It was a gesture that made him look for all the world like a horse. 'Don't worry, dear boy. Spinner poison doesn't work as quickly as I said – that was purely in the hope of obtaining a little more hard cash. A difficult commodity for a man in my position these days, I fear.' He stopped licking his teeth long enough to suck them. 'However, we do have a small problem. There is no known antidote to spinner venom.'

Marcus groaned inwardly. So there was no hope after all. But somehow he didn't care. He had passed beyond fear into a place where all he wanted was for the nightmare to end, even if it ended in death.

'Thus,' Master Squat was saying, 'since we cannot neutralize the poison, we needs must remove it.' He reached down and in one deft movement rolled Marcus on to his face, then slid off his jerkin. Marcus, with his face pressed against the lumpy covering of the couch and his mouth half-full of horse-hair, heard him drop the jacket on the floor and move away. There was the squeak of a hinge as the surgeon's cabinet was opened.

'You see,' said Master Squat, 'your friends may not be your friends after all. That coarse fellow who carried you in here does not believe I have the skill to cure you, that's for certain. Why then did he bring you? Why then did he donate hard-earned coin to help pay a portion of my fee? Because, dear boy, he thought if you must die, it would be better if you died here. For then the blame, if blame there be, would lie at my door. A cunning person, Master Morrigam.'

Unable to move, Marcus wondered if it might be true. Strang Morrigam had always been a decent enough Master, but soft cheese was hard won and every man must look to his own interests first.

'Ah, my beauties,' Squat murmured as he walked back again. 'Time to do your work.' He began to pull up Marcus's shirt. 'But we may trick him yet, young Mustard. This will not hurt. Well, scarcely at all. But I should warn you that you will feel very weak afterwards – weak and tired. Quite normal, I assure you, but worrying if you were not expecting it.'

Marcus felt something wet placed on his naked back to one side of the spine, then another just below the wound on his shoulder where the spinner sank her claw. Three more went on at different spots, including one tucked under his left arm. It felt about the size of a plum, but damp, soft and cold – like a leech.

'Now, dear boy, lie still and let my pets do their appointed work.'

Lie still, Marcus thought sourly. What option had he? There was, as promised, no pain; no feeling of any sort really. Even the damp chill faded in a moment or two. He waited. Still nothing.

'I shall now go about my business,' Squat said, 'if you will excuse me. But fear not, I shall look in on you from time to time.'

There was the swish of the curtain as he went into the shop. As Marcus's open eyes focused on the filthy fabric of the couch, he felt a pall of gloom descend. Had he offended the Mother and her Holy Twins to find himself in such a state? Or had he fallen foul of darker gods? And what had Master Squat done to him? Whatever had been placed under his arm seemed bigger now and warmer. Marcus thought it might be pulsing, but could not be sure.

He felt tired, as Master Squat had predicted, and his tiredness increased as the thing beneath his arm grew larger still. He found his thoughts drifting, as if he were passing into sleep.

Squat's voice came to him as if from a great distance. 'Ah, cooking nicely, I see. Yes, indeed, my lovelies, what a marvellous job you are doing. Sleep if you can, Prentice Mustard. You will be hungry when you waken.'

Sleep if he could? Just now it was all he could do to stay awake. He felt exhaustion roll over him in waves and shifted his position slightly to make himself more comfortable on the lumpy couch. He wondered what it was Master Squat had placed upon him. He wondered if there was even a small chance the treatment might work. He wondered—

He had shifted his position! He had *moved*!

The realization sent such an explosion of excitement through him that he almost called aloud to Master Squat. But though he could move his body a little now, he still could not move his tongue at all. He tried to shout, but all he heard was an outbreath and a rasping, sighing grunt. Exhaustion still gripped him, tiredness still rolled over him, breaking his excitement into little bubbles which popped and disappeared, one after another.

'Mm,' murmured Marcus Mustard sleepily as his eyes at last slid closed.

He awoke in a soft bed, staring at a strange ceiling in a bright room. His first thought was of something missing. There was no longer a lump beneath his arm, but that was not it. Something else . . . something not to do with anything he . . . He had it! He did not hear the singing! For the first time in days he had awakened without the sound of singing.

Had the spinner venom changed him in some way? He supposed it must have, although he felt well enough. Very well, in fact. But oddly, for it had only come to him a week ago, he found he missed the singing.

Marcus sat up and felt his head spin alarmingly. He waited for it to settle, then took stock. He was in a high bed – the first real bed he'd ever slept in – in a small, bright room with a single window. There was no other furniture save a smallish table on which stood an unlit lamp, but the floorboards were covered by a scattering of rugs. They were old, well-worn and threadbare, but they were still far more than he had ever seen in any dormitory or bedroom in his life.

He felt weak and ravenously hungry, but he could move every finger, every toe; could waggle his tongue, wrinkle his nose, even twitch his ears a little. Whatever Master Squat had done had rid his system of the spinner poison.

He was naked, but his clothes lay in a heap beside the bed. He climbed out carefully, wrapping one of the blankets—

(*this bed had blankets, threadbare like the rugs, but real blankets all the same, not old smelly hides*)

—round his shoulders, and walked unsteadily to the window.

He was in an upstairs garret. The window looked down on the street where a group of brown-robed pilgrims was marching in the morning sun. He watched them for a moment as they broke into a lively chant. They looked excited enough to be going to the Refreshing, except that the Refreshing was still two days away.

His stomach growled.

It was difficult to be sure, but he thought it

was the same street where Strang Morrigam had brought him in the dog-cart, which meant he was still in the house of Master Squat – probably in a room above the shop. Despite his weakness, he felt a bubble of sheer joy rising from his stomach. He could move! He was well again! He had been poisoned by a spinner and survived! Did that not mean the Mother and her Holy Twins must favour him? He smiled down at the pilgrims, but none looked up to see him.

What now? He remembered Master Morrigam's parting words. *You get him cured, you tell him to walk back to the silk pits and sharpish.* Well, he was cured for sure, but he didn't think he was ready to walk back to the silk pits yet. He glanced round at the bed. He could scarcely believe any sleeping place could be so soft. What he wanted was to climb back into that bed and curl up and sleep again until the Master Wranglers grew tired of waiting and sent for him or, better still, forgot him altogether. He did not want to go back to the pits and the webs and the spinners with the poison in their claws.

His stomach growled again, then contracted violently. More than sleep in a soft bed, he wanted food. He was ravenous, weak from hunger. He thought of going downstairs to seek out Master Squat, perhaps beg a crust of bread from him or a piece of dried fish. At the thought, his hunger became an urgency.

He pulled on shirt and breeches like a boy demented and headed for the door without bothering to put on his boots. He was actually on the landing outside when he remembered. He still had the square of cheese in the pocket of his jerkin!

Marcus tumbled back into the room. He was so

hungry now his hand was shaking as he fumbled for the cheese. It was still there, along with his useless spellbell! As he took the cheese out, he could smell it through the muslin wrapping.

He flung the muslin on to the little table and bit into the cheese. It was the best he had ever tasted. He could not imagine that Lord Dark, the Alizarin Emperor himself, ate better off his golden plates. Drooling uncontrollably, he wolfed it down, then licked his fingers to make sure he did not miss a single crumb.

He was still hungry, but the cheese had stopped him shaking. He slid into his jerkin and bent to pull on his boots. As he did so, he noticed the muslin he had thrown aside and suddenly remembered the writing he had seen on it while hanging close to death above the silk pits. Curiously he picked it up.

The writing was ill-formed, but clear enough. It said:

Marcus Mustard,

Fain Would I Be Thy Special Friend.

It was not signed, but it could only have been written by Prudence Rainwater.

Chapter Five

The crowds were so dense he could hardly push his way through; and when he reached the square, he found out why. The players from the North Tower were in mid-performance, with a retinue of cartmen, hawkers, traymen, buskers and beggars ringed around. There would be cut-purses and pickpockets working this crowd as well, Marcus thought. Not that he was worried. He had spent his money, eaten his cheese and lost his 'prentice knife, so the only thing left in his pocket was his broken spellbell and any thief was welcome to that.

He looked around and spotted the high arch across the northern entrance to the square. There were half a dozen children there already and Marcus climbed to join them. They were younger than he was, so they moved over without fuss. He sat, legs dangling.

'What be happening?' he asked the nearest child – an urchin so filthy black he could only be a sweep's assistant.

The youngster never took his wide eyes off the players. 'They're doing the story of the 'Freshing. Hawksmore and his Lady will be coming in a minute.'

Marcus grinned to himself. There was not a soul in Castle Dis who did not know the story of the Refreshing. It began in the days of the second sun when the tribe of Dis were nomads wandering the face of Pradesh. Their greatest enemies, the Tarquish, mounted a surprise attack which proved so successful that one third of the men of Dis were killed. King-Hero Ansalom of Dis realized his people could not long survive such slaughter and ordered special fortifications to be built around their nomadic yurt dwellings.

The plan worked. The first wooden fortifications repelled the Tarquish for forty days and forty nights before they finally broke through. But by that time, the wily Ansalom had built a second line of fortifications in brick. It took the Tarquish seven moons to break through those and by the time they did, a third line of defence had been built in stone.

There were some who believed the stone fortifications would be enough to win the war, but King Ansalom was not among them. *Soft cheese is hard won*, he told his people and set them to building a keep behind the walls and a castle around the keep. In time the castle grew to be the largest, strongest, most impregnable fortress on the face of their world. Castle Dis stretched so far that a man on horseback would take days to ride from one corner of it to the other. The Tarquish, seeing such a stronghold, realized they could never win. They withdrew their armies and sued for peace.

For a time everyone was happy. But the people of Dis were nomads at heart and missed the freedom of travelling from place to place. Soon there was so much muttered discontent that Ansalom lived in fear of being murdered in the night. He dug a great labyrinth of passages and pits beneath his mighty castle and hid there with his Queen and family while rioting and looting broke out in the castle streets.

Then, just as things reached desperation, a great

light appeared in the eastern sky and beneath it, Lord Hawksmore and his Lady rode up to the gates of Castle Dis. Lord Hawksmore was a wizard and his Lady was a witch, so they knew exactly where the King was hiding and went to him at once.

In audience with Ansalom, they proposed a bargain. The King must agree to the establishment of a Guild of Wizards, headed by Hawksmore and his Lady, who would have control of all magic used in Castle Dis. Hawksmore, for his part, would undertake to cast a mighty spell which would lift the entire castle and place it on a new and distant part of Pradesh when the people grew restless.

The King agreed and ordained that the mighty spell would henceforth and forever be known as the Refreshing, for it refreshed the spirit of his people. He requested that the Wizard Hawksmore ensure the castle came to rest at each of the seven sacred sites of Dis people. So it was that the Refreshing transported the castle in rotation to Lipslade Steppe, the Mare Sirenas, Jubal Distala, Four Corms Bite, Rhymmer Porcorum, Dragonhead Flay and Mandrake Forest Deep.

When the King announced what was to happen, the people were delighted and returned to their homes. But after the first Refreshing, when the castle moved from Lipslade Steppe to the tranquil shores of the Mare Sirenas, the people found they had no land of their own to grow crops and no goods to trade with the Siren people of the sea.

Soon the residents of Dis grew hungry and renewed murmurings began, not alone against their King, but against the newly formed Guild of

Wizards, which had taken over all the magic in the castle. So Lord Hawksmore's Lady turned herself into a spinner and went to live in the labyrinth of pits and tunnels where the King had once hidden. There she spun her silk to be harvested and turned into cloth for trade with all those who came to Dis following a Refreshing. Because of her sacrifice, prosperity returned to Castle Dis and the descendants of the Lady Hawksmore lived in the silk pits beneath Dis to this day.

It was all a story, of course. When he became an apprentice wrangler, Marcus learned the truth. Well before the advent of Lord Hawksmore and the Wizards' Guild, an explorer named Scrof the Younger had discovered spinners in a weird volcanic wasteland somewhere to the north.

Scrof named this inhospitable place the *Pooka Ginid*, or Land of Sprites and Spirits, on account of its desolation. Sheer cliffs cut it off from the rest of the world. Only luck had shown Scrof a way in. The climate was dismal, like much of Northern Pradesh, but the temperature was unusually high, on account of the volcanic fumaroles and springs. Twisted plants, found nowhere else, grew there.

Scrof arrived at the Pooka Ginid in winter. When he left, he carried back to the Tribe of Dis examples of strange fruits, plants and seeds, a great many crystals, a dozen eggs from several thousand he had discovered in a cave, and what he believed to be a sample of ore-bearing rock.

It was the rock that excited him, for he thought the ore was gold. But it was the eggs that made him famous. They lay dormant throughout his journey home, but on the first day of the summer following his arrival, three of them hatched into spinners.

Scrof was not there to see it. He had raised

money for another expedition north and had the misfortune to reach his destination in late spring. A week after he got there, a torrent of hatchling spinners flooded from the caverns of the Pooka Ginid and ate him. According to the only one of his companions to escape, none was larger than a mouse.

This, Marcus knew, was the reality of it. The spinners of Dis had nothing to do with magic or the Lady Hawksmore. They were bred from the three that Scrof had left behind.

But the romantic Hawksmore legend was much more entertaining and many children believed it to be true. Marcus looked out towards the players as a tall, golden-haired actor in the formal toga of a wizard strode into the square. At his elbow was a woman of such beauty that Marcus found himself holding his breath. She must have been a remarkable actress as well, for he thought of the spinners the moment he looked at her. Perhaps it was something in the way she moved.

'Hawksmore! Hawksmore! Hawksmore!' the crowd began to chant. It was the traditional response at this point in the play.

'Hawksmore!' shouted the soot-blackened urchin excitedly. He turned to Marcus. 'Ain't she lovely – the wizard's lady?'

'She be that for sure,' Marcus agreed.

The youngster blinked. 'Cor,' he said, 'you don't half talk funny.'

Marcus smiled at him without replying. Talk funny he might, but just now he was glad to be able to talk at all. He could hardly believe his luck. He suspected even Master Squat might have been surprised by so fast a recovery, although it was difficult to know what Master Squat thought of

44

anything just now. When Marcus had gone to thank him, he was dead drunk on sembala juice.

'Your Majesty,' called the golden-haired actor to the player who was King Ansalom, 'my Lady and I have travelled far from Lobal Ling, the Land of Mystery and Magic, that we might visit mighty Castle Dis, herein to—'

Marcus felt excited by the words, as he felt excited by all the ancient tales of Castle Dis. He wished he could stay to watch the rest of the performance, but knew he could not. Indeed, he should not have stopped at all. He had missed an entire morning's work and the Master Wranglers would not look too kindly on him if he missed any more, even if he had been poisoned by a spinner.

He watched a little while longer, then began to slide sideways so he could climb down from the arch.

'You off then?' the urchin asked suspiciously.

'Aye,' Marcus nodded. He swung over the edge with the easy gait of one accustomed to walking the webs.

'Mind out for the guards,' the youngster said. 'Lot of them about today.'

Marcus dropped down into the crowd and began to push his way out of the square. Since he could not get across while the players performed, he would have to cut through the alleyway between the Weavers' Guildhall and the grain store. That would take him into Quarterstaff Court, where he could get on to The Cut and hence into Falcon Street and the Trade Road. Once there, it was no more than a mile to Dead Man's Bite, which was the nearest entrance to the silk pits. If he ran part of the way, none of the Masters would suspect he had stopped off to watch the players, even should they ever think to ask Master Squat what time he set out. Not that Master Squat would know in any case.

The Cut was almost empty when he reached it – a rare occurrence. He was halfway across when he heard the sound of marching feet.

Marcus glanced behind him. A small contingent of guards had entered The Cut, walking four abreast. They all looked as if they had been snipped from the same cloth – hard-muscled, broad-shouldered men in the distinctive black leather armour of their profession. More than half of them sported heavy moustaches. A few had beards.

He looked away quickly. It never did to catch the eye of guards, even when you had done nothing. They were short-tempered by nature and trained to suspicion. Not that he thought he had much to worry on. They would have little to do if they decided to question a fourteen-year-old 'prentice. All the same, he quickened his step. There were many stories of the guards, few of them pleasant. Some claimed they beat people for fun.

'Hey!' a harsh voice called behind him. 'Hey, you!'

It would not be him. Or perhaps it *was* him. Perhaps they wondered why a 'prentice would be wandering the streets when he should be working in the pits. Except that any 'prentice was entitled to leave the pits after his shift once he had worked there for a year. So it would not be him.

'You, boy – I'm talking to you!'

Marcus glanced back again nervously. The leader of the guards, a burly man with a sergeant's insignia, was waving in his direction. Was there anyone near that the man might be waving at? There was no-one near.

'Yes, you! The horrible little slug with the red hair!' the guard roared. 'Stand still and don't move!'

Marcus ran. He knew that men in armour – even leather armour – could not stay a running pace for long. Instead of heading into Falcon Street as he had planned, he dodged through the narrow archway and down the short flight of stone steps which led into Chesterfield Market. Even with players in the square, he reckoned the market would draw enough trade to let him slip away in the crowd. There was no reason for the guards to stop him, no reason at all, and so he would not be stopped. He doubted the Sergeant had seen his face long enough to know him again.

He burst out of the alleyway into the market and careered straight into a trayman.

'What you think you're at, you little maggot?' the trayman snarled. 'Nearly had my pies on the cobbles.' He grabbed Marcus by the shoulder, just where the spinner sank her claw. To Marcus's surprise, it hardly hurt at all.

'Sorry,' Marcus gasped. He struggled to get away, but could not. The aroma of boiled beef and onions floated from the tray, setting his stomach into fresh ferment.

'What's your hurry anyway?' the pieman asked. He was a balding man of about forty with close-set eyes.

Marcus decided to tell the truth. 'Guards be after me, good sir.' It was small risk. There were few in this part of Castle Dis who sided with the guards.

'What you done then?' the trayman asked suspiciously.

'Nothing, by my life,' Marcus swore.

'By your life, is it? Might be if those lads get their hands on you.' He sniffed. 'You a 'prentice then?'

'So I be,' said Marcus, with just a note of pride. 'Prenticed to the silk trade.' He was not allowed to mention the spinners, although it was an open secret in the castle itself. Lord Dark, the Alizarin Emperor, had decreed that none outside the Tribe of Dis should learn how the silk was produced. He feared to lose the castle's monopoly on the trade. A man might only be jailed for murder, unless he killed a noble. He could be hanged for stealing spinner eggs.

'Aren't we all,' the pieman said obscurely. From the alleyway behind there came the heavy sound of boots on stone, running. He released his grip abruptly. 'Better be off then, since you done nothing.'

Marcus snatched a pie from the tray as he dived into the market throng.

'Here!' shouted the trayman furiously. But before he could do anything else, the guards were pouring into the market, spinning him round so that all his goods went flying. He broke into a stream of curses.

Marcus crammed pie into his mouth as he ran, weaving in and out of the crowds. Gravy dripped down his chin, but he ignored it. The pie was the best he had ever eaten – short, thick pastry over soft-boiled beef, carrots, leeks and onions; holiday fare although the 'Freshing was still two days off. He was far less worried about the guards now than he had been at The Cut. He was a broad enough boy, but far from tall. If he was careful, there was no way they would see him in the market throng.

All he had to do was make his way quietly to one of the exits and . . .

He was approaching an exit now, but stopped in time, guards were pouring into the market from that street too. Marcus looked around and chilled. There seemed to be more guards coming in at every exit. Why? For so many guards there had to be a magical Calling, which was always expensive. Certainly no Sergeant would dare put out a Calling just for the pleasure of harassing a 'prentice. Maybe he had been wrong. Maybe, despite all appearances, they were after somebody else.

He noticed one archway which was free of guards. It led into a short tunnel which, so far as he remembered, emerged into Abacus Lane. It would do him well enough. Even if they weren't after him, he would feel better well away from them. Besides, he still had to get back to his work. There was another entrance to the silk pits near the Mutton Market and he could get there from Abacus Lane.

Marcus made one last check on the guards, then dived into the gloomy archway. His footsteps echoed in the tunnel, then he was back in the sunlight again on Abacus Lane. He grinned to himself and stuffed away the last of the pie.

'Gotcha!' growled a deep voice in his ear.

'What do you want, good sirs?' Marcus screamed as his arms were pinned. 'What have I done?'

He was surrounded by black-armoured guards and more were arriving every minute. 'Stole a pie, for one thing,' grinned one of them. He stroked his moustache. 'Could get your hand chopped off for that, you could.'

Marcus kicked and struggled, then twisted his

49

head to bite the hands that pinned him. But it was hopeless. The guard who had him was an expert.

The men around him parted respectfully as the big Sergeant who had first spotted him pushed through. 'Not as smart as you thought, eh, Ginger,' he said thoughtfully. He nodded to one of his men. 'Get the manacles on, Jar. And put a chain through them. Slippery customer we got here.'

'I bain't done nothing!' Marcus protested as the metal manacles went round his wrists. Jar placed a second pair above his ankles and joined them with a chain.

'Maybe you have and maybe you haven't,' the Sergeant said. 'You're Marcus Mustard, aren't yer?'

Marcus stared at him in astonishment. Until that moment he had still been half convinced the guards had made a mistake. Now he realized they had been after him all along. But why? The last time he had seen so many guards, they had been protecting the Alizarin Emperor himself in a State Progression.

'You're Mustard, right enough,' the Sergeant said. 'Can see it in your face.' He turned away. 'Keep him between you, lads. Make sure the little bleeder doesn't get away, but mind you don't hurt him too much either. Boss wants to see him in one piece.' He threw out his chest. 'By the right . . . *quick march!*''

Marcus marched with them out of Abacus Lane and into Cheapside, then on to Mapstone's Mall, Smithy Place, Smithy Street, Cockroyd Terrace and on to a street he did not know. Within minutes he was in an unfamiliar district of the castle – one where the buildings looked better than anything he was used to near the silk pits.

'Left turn!' the Sergeant commanded.

The guards swung left and stopped outside a building with an overhanging balcony. There were curious symbols cut into the pillars by the door. Marcus noticed there was neither knocker nor bell chain, but set into the door at shoulder height was a square plate of what seemed to be polished obsidian. The Sergeant placed his hand firmly on the glistening surface. At once the familiar scent of magic filled the air, like the smell of a bellspell, but far deeper and more pungent.

There was no sound, but after a moment the door swung open.

'Lose your fingers if you tried that without authorization,' whispered one of the guards on Marcus's right. He was looking with admiration at the Sergeant.

'Bring him in, lads,' the Sergeant said. 'We're expected.'

As Marcus was manhandled forward, he realized suddenly where they were taking him. The building with the obsidian plate in its door was headquarters of the Wizards' Guild.

Chapter Six

Like everyone else in Dis, Marcus Mustard had heard stories about the Wizards' Guildhall. Every room was decorated by hanging gardens floating ten feet from the floor. You entered through a mirror maze which always guided you towards the person you needed to see. There were corridors patrolled by manticores. One chamber housed a talking bat.

The reality was different and a little frightening. The guards marched him directly to an enormous reception hall. There were neither chairs nor any other furnishing, but to one side, only a few feet away, rose a thick pillar which stopped just short of the ceiling.

Flanked by two guards, Marcus was half turned, staring woodenly towards it. The pillar was not made from stone or any other building material he could recognize. If he had not known better, he might even have imagined it was made from water, for its surface shimmered and whirled in constant, fluid motion. He pulled his eyes away with an effort.

After a time, the waiting grew too much for him. 'Sergeant Master, sir,' he said to the broad back of the Sergeant, who now stood uneasily at attention directly in front of him. 'What's to happen here?'

'Shut it!' hissed the Sergeant out the side of his mouth. 'You'll find out soon enough.'

Marcus turned back to the squat pillar. The

guards were the law in Castle Dis. They picked you up and took you in and questioned you. If they were satisfied you'd misbehaved, they punished you: a birching for a 'prentice who should have been at work, slit nostrils for a cut-purse to mark him, five days' dungeons for a nagging wife, three for the husband who beat her. And on, all the way to hanging. All the penalties were set out in the Alizarin Code, but it was the guards who decided if you were guilty. They answered only to their officers and could question almost anyone, anywhere, at any time. It made them probably the most hated group in the castle.

But they were not all-powerful. They were not allowed to question the nobility at all, let alone punish them. And like everyone else, commoner or noble, they went in mortal fear of wizards. So why had they brought him to the Wizards' Guildhall?

He turned back to the burly Sergeant. 'Sir—' A flicker caught his eye. Marcus jerked round and his question turned into a gasping cry. *There was something inside the pillar!* It glared malevolently and raked the inside surface with powerful claws. It stood as high as a man, higher than some, but had the wire-frame body of an insect – black, glistening and naked beneath a floor-length cloak.

The face was like nothing he had ever seen, like nothing he ever wished to see again. It was a woman's face, or the face of a pretty man, plump, pale and flabby with a tiny rose-bud mouth. It was the most unholy thing he could imagine attached to that ghastly body. The creature seemed to be screaming hatred as it clawed at the inside of the pillar, but no sound emerged.

'What is it now?' the Sergeant growled impatiently. He half turned towards Marcus, then caught sight of the pillar. 'No need to let yer kidneys run away, boy – it's a demon, but it can't get out.' He turned back and resumed his rigid pose.

Marcus shivered uncontrollably but could not take his eyes away from the creature in the pillar. The spinners were ugly, but this thing was simply *wrong*. To look at it was to feel sick in the stomach. He found himself wondering if this was what the priests meant when they talked of living blasphemies.

The demon clawed and writhed. For an instant it stared deep into Marcus's eyes so that he could almost taste its hunger for his soul. The rosebud mouth opened to reveal two rows of tiny pearl-white teeth, each filed (or growing!) to a point. The thing raised insect arms and beat at the pillar which confined it. Then, abruptly, it was gone and he was staring once again at swirling, liquid fog. He felt his knees tremble. What breed of mortal men were wizards who could keep a demon caged so casually in their reception hall?

'How do they feed it?' Marcus whispered, as much to himself as anyone else.

The Sergeant ignored him, but the guard on his right, who was even nearer the pillar than he was, murmured, 'Don't have to. That's a shaft, not a box. Goes all the way down.'

Marcus swallowed. 'To . . . the *Chaos Hells*?' he asked, eyes wide with disbelief. The Chaos Hells were the world of demons, according to the priests and Bishop Puddifat. Good men were supposed to steer clear of them, not drive down shafts so demons could peer out at the world of humankind.

Marcus felt a sudden tension in the guards as a door at the far side of the chamber burst open. A fat man with a wide mouth bustled in. 'Sergeant Ireland, do we have him?'

Marcus craned round the bulk of the Sergeant. The fat man was wearing floor-length robes of finest spinner silk! It was a garment worth an emperor's ransom. Around his throat was a necklace of eight enormous polished gems which glittered darkly, changing from pearl grey to deepest black like spinner's eyes. Even the nobility Marcus saw in State Progressions were not so richly dressed. Yet this man wore his finery casually, as if it were nothing at all special.

'Yes, sir,' the Sergeant said stiffly.

'Then where is he, dear Sergeant? Where are you, young Mustard? I must see you. I must talk to you. There is no time to waste!'

'Yes, sir. Sorry, sir.' The Sergeant stepped quickly to one side and half turned. 'This is him, sir.'

Marcus watched open-mouthed as the fat man bore down. He was not particularly tall, only an inch or two above Marcus, in fact, but the folds of fat on his body wobbled when he walked, causing the robes to slide and shimmer. The odd thing was that he moved swiftly, as light on his feet as a chicken.

'Prentice Mustard, sweet boy! How good of you to come!' To Marcus's astonishment, the fat man flung his arms around him and embraced him fondly. Then he stepped back and held Marcus at arm's length, cocking his head to one side to

55

study him. 'What a handsome boy. So broad, so strong, such fine red hair. And working to become a Master Wrangler! Such ambition!' He wagged a finger like a sausage in Marcus's face. 'But you will achieve it. You will do well. I predict it absolutely.' He smiled benignly. 'What is your given name, dear boy? I cannot bear to call you Prentice Mustard as if we are not friends.'

Marcus blinked. 'Marcus,' he said.

'Sudswarts,' exclaimed the fat man. 'But you must call me Ansalom.' He put his arm around Marcus's shoulders as the guards exchanged side-long glances. 'I was named for our first Emperor, King Ansalom. You've heard of him, no doubt.' He smiled broadly and giggled, like one who is making a joke. 'Better I should have been Hawksmore, eh? More appropriate.'

Hawksmore, the first wiz—? The name Sudswarts suddenly sank in and it was like an explosion inside Marcus's head. The Wizard Sudswarts! Not just the first wizard he had ever met face to face, but Sudswarts, the Chairman of the Wizards' Guild. The First Wizard of Dis. This little fat man in the expensive robes was almost as powerful as Lord Dark, the Alizarin Emperor. In some ways *more* powerful.

'Yes, Master,' Marcus said, jaw hanging.

'Now, Marcus,' Sudswarts said, 'you're a brave boy, I'm sure of that. I heard all about your little adventure with the spinner, you know. Now we must find out how observant you are.' He was guiding Marcus gently across the floor. 'I should very much like you to tell me about it.'

'And the sooner the better,' a cold voice said.

A second man had entered the room, dressed in the formal linen toga of a wizard. He was tall as

Sudswarts was short – thin as he was fat. Ice-dark eyes stared out from an unsmiling face, reminding Marcus of a predatory spinner.

'Oh, but he will, Alan,' Sudswarts said in a relaxed conciliatory tone. 'I'm certain he will – such a fine boy.' He turned, his arm still around Marcus's shoulders, his left hand fingering the gemstone necklace. 'This is Lord Alan Ruslan, Marcus. I'm sure you'll be friends with him as well.'

The Wizard Earl. He was looking at the Wizard Earl! Women made warding signs when a carriage passed with his insignia. Not one in a thousand knew what he looked like, but all knew his chilling reputation.

'I doubt it,' Ruslan said dryly, apparently referring to the likelihood that he and Marcus would be friends.

'Well, perhaps, perhaps not,' said Sudswarts. 'In any case, I'm certain Marcus will be of great help in our little difficulties. Great, great help. Won't you, dear boy?'

'I don't know, Master,' Marcus told him honestly. He hardly knew what was going on, let alone what the First Wizard was talking about.

'Good, good,' said Sudswarts as if he had not heard. Over his shoulder he said, 'Take your men through to the kitchens, Sergeant. I'm sure they're hungry after all that searching. My secretary will let you have a little something for your trouble before you leave.'

'Yes, sir,' the Sergeant said stiffly.

Sudswarts bustled Marcus into a small ante-room. 'Take that chair, dear boy – it's terribly comfortable.'

The chair looked like an ordinary armchair, but

as soon as Marcus sat, it moulded itself around his buttocks and began, gently, to massage his back. Marcus squeaked in alarm and jumped up again.

Even the saturnine Ruslan allowed himself a thin smile. 'You will become accustomed to it, 'Prentice. You may even learn to like it.'

Marcus sat down again gingerly. The chair seemed to wriggle against him, embrace him with its arms. After a moment he did indeed start to think of it as pleasant – nerve-wracking, but pleasant. He stared at the two wizards without speaking. First Wizard Sudswarts took a second chair similar to his own. The Wizard Earl, he noticed, remained standing.

Sudswarts leaned forward. 'Now, sweet boy, we know how dreadful it must have been for you to have been almost . . . well, *eaten* by a spinner. Quite, quite *dreadful*. I could never have stood it myself. And I'm certain you must want to put it from your mind so desperately. But there are times, dear boy, when duty must come first – when one must put the welfare of one's fellows, the welfare of Castle Dis, before one's own. I—'

'He wants you to tell him what happened,' the Wizard Earl Ruslan put in.

Sudswarts glared at him. 'Sometimes, Alan, you are almost *crass*.' But he swung his gaze back to Marcus expectantly.

Marcus swallowed. 'The spinner clawed me on the arm and shoulder. This arm—' He pointed. 'She poisoned me and fixed a cable and—'

'No, no, dear boy – *before* that. We're aware the spinner moved. We want to know about before that.'

'The spellbell,' Ruslan put in. His eyes were like those of a reptile.

'It didn't work,' Marcus said, bewildered.

'Didn't work?' Sudswarts was like a spinner pouncing on its prey. 'You mean it didn't chime?'

'No, sir. It chimed, but it didn't work. I mean, it *seemed* to work. The spinner froze same as always, else I wouldn't have gone on the web.' Marcus stared at them, wide-eyed. 'Only she didn't stay froze, sirs.'

'Are you sure you rang the bell at all?' Ruslan asked coldly.

Sudswarts rounded on him. 'Of *course* he rang the bell! Does he look like a fool?'

'Yes,' said Ruslan bluntly.

Sudswarts looked back at Marcus. 'Well, perhaps.' He hesitated, then added, 'Perhaps not. I don't believe you forgot to ring the bell. You didn't forget, did you, Marcus?'

'No.'

'No,' Sudswarts echoed. 'Of course not. But think well, Marcus. The bell definitely did chime?'

'Aye, Master.'

Sudswarts would not let it alone. 'You know what happens when a spellbell runs out of magic, don't you, Marcus? They must have taught you that.'

'It don't chime, Master,' Marcus said. 'It's wore out. Broke.'

'And you have experience of a broken spellbell?' Ruslan put in.

'I be 'prentice near two year, Master,' Marcus told him. It was answer enough. Everyone knew the Wizards' Guild made spellbells to last six months and not a day longer.

'So this one was not broken?' Ruslan insisted. 'It definitely sounded its usual chime when you used it?'

'Yes sir.' He wondered why the interest in the spellbell; why he was here at all.

'And it was the *usual* chime?' Sudswarts asked. 'It didn't sound any different to you?'

'How, different?' Marcus frowned.

'Louder. Softer. Different note. How should I know, different? That's what I'm asking you.'

Marcus thought for a moment, then shook his head. 'Didn't sound no different to any other times, Masters. You can listen for yourself if you don't believe me.'

Sudswarts sat up as if bitten. 'You still have the bell?' When Marcus nodded, he said, 'I thought you'd dropped it in the pit.' He glanced across at Ruslan. 'Idiots told me he'd dropped it in the pit.' He looked back at Marcus. 'You didn't drop it in the pit?'

'No, Master.'

'You have it with you? Now?'

'Yes, Master.'

'Give it here!' Sudswarts ordered impatiently. Then, as Marcus fished the bell from his pocket, 'Oh, you dear, dear boy!' He snatched the artefact from Marcus's hand and swung it violently. No chime emerged. He looked at Marcus accusingly. 'It doesn't sound!' He raised the bell above his head to look inside it. 'Well, no wonder it doesn't sound – there's something stuffed inside.' Fat fingers dipped in to extract a wad of muslin.

'That be mine,' said Marcus hurriedly.

But Sudswarts was already frowning at the muslin. 'Someone's been writing on this. *Marcus*

60

Mustard, fain would I be thy special friend. What's all that about?'

Ruslan stopped Marcus's deepening embarrassment by cutting in. 'For heaven's sake, Ansalom, the boy has some wench sweet on him, that's all. Not everyone's as you are, you know. Test the bell.'

'Oh yes,' Sudswarts said absently. He swung the bell again. It rang with a sweet, clear chime. 'Sounds fine to me.' He began turning it over in his hands, as if searching for a secret rune on its surface.

'Like the others,' Ruslan sighed. 'Looks fine, sounds fine, but sometimes doesn't work.'

Sudswarts glanced at him in alarm. 'Quiet! Little jugs have great big handles.'

'For heaven's sake,' the Earl Ruslan groaned impatiently, 'the boy's an idiot – anyone can see that. What does he understand about the subtleties of magic? And what more harm will it do us if he could? It's only a matter of time before everybody knows. The fabric's tearing, Sudswarts. You've said as much yourself for weeks. Soon you won't know when a spell will work at all, and what will happen to our income then? Who will pay the Wizards' Guild to make a spell that might only work sometimes and give no warning of its failure?'

'Well, you've told him now,' said Sudswarts petulantly. 'Perhaps he is an idiot, and perhaps not. But I certainly can't have him spreading it around that you can't trust magic any more – and straight from the horse's mouth, so to speak. Straight from the Wizard Earl himself. No, sir. Thanks to your loose tongue, we'll have to keep him here.'

61

'We were planning that in any case, you may recall,' said Ruslan coldly.

'Only until after tonight's Refreshing,' Sudswarts said. 'Only until we were sure we'd found out all he knew!'

Marcus felt his head go in a spin. Whatever Ruslan thought, he was no idiot. These men were saying his spellbell wasn't the first to go wrong. It sounded as if magic had been failing them in little ways for weeks. But magic *never* failed. It *had* to work reliably, otherwise the whole life of Castle Dis would fall apart. One spellbell failing was a mystery. But if other spells were failing too, that had the makings of a disaster. And no-one had more to lose than the wizards, who were paid highly to make sure that magic worked. No wonder the First Wizard and the Wizard Earl had been so keen to see him. Any new report of magic failure must send them scurrying in panic now.

But what was far worse than the thought of magic failing were the clear signs that these great wizards were trying desperately to keep it secret. They seemed more concerned that people should trust magic than that people could no longer use it safely. How many 'prentices were ringing spellbells and climbing unto spinner webs as they talked? How many workmen were stepping on to magic scaffolds? How many doctors trusting magic cures? People could *die* if they used magic and it didn't work.

'Well,' sighed Sudswarts, standing up abruptly, 'I don't suppose he'll tell us much more now you've spilled the beans. I'll have that nice Sergeant throw him in the dungeons until we decide what must be done with him. Meanwhile—' He dropped the spellbell into a pocket of his robes.

'—we need to have this fully tested.' He swept out. Ruslan followed without a word.

For the barest second Marcus hesitated, then dived for the door himself. Or at least tried to. As he began to move, his chair gripped him firmly. Struggle as he might, he could not break free.

He was still struggling vainly when he heard the sound of marching feet. As Sergeant Ireland and his men tramped in, it dawned on Marcus that First Wizard Sudswarts had said the Refreshing was tonight. Which meant today was Thorsday and he had not slept a few hours at the house of Master Squat, but two whole days.

At another time this might have panicked him completely. Now he had a lot more on his mind as the black-armoured guards dragged him from his treacherous chair and marched him, struggling, down the steep stone steps into the darkness of the dungeons beneath the Wizards' Guild.

Chapter Seven

Marcus awoke to singing, real but faint, like sounds coming from a distance. As always, it faded soon after he opened his eyes. He moved stiffly. His body ached and there was a smell of vermin from his straw bed, but his mind was alert. Despite his circumstances, he felt an undercurrent of joy – the result of the Refreshing, which had taken place in the night. Everyone felt good after a Refreshing, at least for a while.

He looked around. He was sorry he had missed the 'Freshing celebrations. There would have been jugglers, tumblers and fire-eaters as well as Bishop Puddifat's boring religious parade. Not that the Masters always allowed him to join in the fun – if a 'prentice happened to be working night shift, he missed it altogether – but he had been looking forward to this one until his troubles started.

The thought of his troubles quickly ate through the joy. He was in big trouble, no mistake. He was locked in a dank, smelly dungeon beneath the Wizards' Guildhall. He was going to be held here until—

The door was ajar!

He climbed hurriedly to his feet and scampered across. He was right! The door was ajar! He moved to open it fully, then hesitated. The door had been firmly locked last night. Why was it open now?

Marcus was a cautious lad. Apprentice wranglers had to be, otherwise they didn't last long in the pits. Caution had given him a suspicious streak and it surfaced now so strongly that his heart began to beat faster. He had heard stories of what happened to awkward prisoners. A cell door would be left 'accidentally' unlocked and any who went through it would be hacked to death 'while trying to escape'. Was this what was planned for him?

He slid to one side of the partly open door and peered through. The corridor seemed empty, but if they were waiting at all, they would be waiting hidden, in ambush. They would not attack until he stepped outside – maybe not until he had gone some distance from his cell.

For a long while he stayed where he was, weighing up what he should do. Then, on an impulse that brushed away caution, he pulled the door and slid out.

No attack came. The corridor really was empty.

Marcus began to move forward. He was in a row of cells, all their doors slightly open. Had they been closed when the guards brought him here? He could not remember. He risked glancing into three of the cells, but they were empty. Perhaps he was the only prisoner beneath the Wizards' Guild that night. Or perhaps the others had wakened earlier and escaped already. Although that would mean all cells had been left unlocked, which seemed unlikely.

He wondered where his jailers had gone. They might have been watching the 'Freshing celebrations last night, but they would have come back long before dawn. Unless, he thought suddenly, he had not slept as long as he imagined and it was still the middle of the night. It was difficult to be sure when you were so deep underground.

The corridor branched and he stood for a

moment, confused. He tried the right fork, but this led him into an open chamber where a pine table showed the remains of a half-eaten supper. On the stone flagging beside it was a short sword.

Marcus stared at it with a tight, mounting excitement. There was not a 'prentice in the pits who could afford a decent dagger, let alone a sword. The Masters issued you with one small, string-bound apprentice knife and that was that. He licked his lips and felt a tingle in the centre of his palm. Should he take it? Like most 'prentices, he never minded stealing things like the pie he pinched from the trayman – but a sword was different. Take a man's sword and you made an enemy for life.

Except that this sword was just lying on the floor.

Marcus picked it up. He had never held a sword before and was surprised how heavy it felt. Heavy, but easy to handle. That would be because of the balance. He had overheard warriors talking about the balance of their weapons and this must be what they meant. He swung the sword and lunged at an imaginary opponent.

Marcus licked his lips again, then chewed the bottom one thoughtfully. He was in trouble already. He could hardly be in any more trouble for stealing a sword. Besides, he might need to protect himself. He waved the sword again, then thrust it into his belt. The weapon had obviously been lost. He would look after it until he found its owner, then he would return it. Yes, that's what he would do.

He left the room by another exit and found himself in a different corridor. More by luck than judgement, he reached the foot of the stairs down which he had been marched the night before. At least, he thought they were the same stairs. He climbed them and discovered they weren't. There was a door at the top in place of an arch, but when he pushed it, it swung open. He emerged into the corridor leading to the Guild front door. If he could only open that, he was free!

Running on tiptoe, Marcus reached the door. It opened at a touch and he shot out like a bolting horse. His best bet was to lose himself in the crowd. Once he blended into the throng of tradesmen and pilgrims he could—

The street was slick with rain, and empty.

Marcus stopped dead. Underground passages and walkways in the depths beneath the castle were sometimes deserted, but he had never seen an open street empty in his life. It unnerved him. Even at dead of night, there were always people moving on the streets of Dis: nobles coming back from parties, bakers making an early start, doctors called to heal the sick, torch-carrying lightermen in search of anyone with a penny to pay for being guided home.

He started to run again. Perhaps the wizards had put some sort of barrier around their Guild-hall. It was possible. Magic was costly for ordinary people. Only nobles could afford it for anything except essentials. But he supposed wizards could use as much as they wanted. They made the spells and set the price.

There was no barrier, magical or otherwise, at the end of Guildhall Street. Marcus emerged into a broad thoroughfare that had to be the Avenue of Ateliers. It was empty too.

He stopped again. The Avenue of Ateliers was never empty. It was one of the main carriage routes to the trade sector of the castle. Every yard of it was jammed with carts and camel-trains and horses, drawing bales of raw silk, finished textiles and Outland goods. Around the caravans were the inevitable hangers-on: traders who sold to the merchants, hawkers who tried to sell to both, draymen, smiths, money chang-ers, porters, roustabouts, spellbinders, guides, lightermen after dark. It was *never* empty.

This couldn't be the Avenue of the Ateliers. He must have made a mistake. But mistake or not, he didn't know of any broad avenue of Castle Dis which would be empty at this time of day. There was a crawling feeling in the pit of his stomach. Something was terribly wrong. He began to walk slowly along the broad, empty street. His footsteps echoed.

He came at length to a street sign. He really was walking the Avenue of the Ateliers. Where were the people?

He turned off and trotted down an (empty!) alley into the Dreaming Promenade, a mean and narrow street despite its name, but one always busy on account of its market. The Dreaming Promenade was as deserted as the Avenue of the Ateliers.

Marcus found he was holding his breath and released it in a long, explosive sigh. The stalls were there, ranged both sides of the Promenade. He walked slowly towards them. There were no stallholders, no customers, but the goods were still on open display. Here was a stall of vegetables, here one of fish, here one of fruit. He picked up a red apple and bit into it absently. No-one called,

Stop thief! There was no-one to pay any attention at all.

He continued walking. Here was a stall of copper pots and pans. Here was a stall of jewellery – not the best, but expensive enough. His hand began to itch again, but he ignored it. He was not a real thief. Snatching an apple was not really thieving. More of a 'prentice game, really. You were birched if you were caught and had to pay for the apple. Just a game. Sometimes you won, sometimes you lost. He would never think of stealing jewellery or anything as valuable as that. The sword in his belt was not really stolen. He was only looking after it for its owner.

It was all so quiet. Marcus had lived his whole life in Castle Dis and had never known quiet until he went underground. Even in the houses, the rumble and chatter of the street was a permanent background. Now everything was still.

Where were the people?

'Hello?' Marcus called and waited.

There was no answer.

He walked further, growing more nervous by the moment, then abruptly took to his heels and ran pell-mell from the market. It began to rain, a light, warm, persistent drizzle as he stumbled into Boxton's Lane (which was empty) and followed it into the empty sweep of Intrinsica Row. There were dog-carts and horse-carts, but neither dogs nor horses; and no people. He saw a wide-brimmed hat lying in the gutter. It looked new. He followed Intrinsica Row all the way to Butchers' Road. Butchers' Road was deserted.

Where were the people? Where . . . he hardly dared think the thought, but thought it all the same . . . where were his friends?

Marcus ran wildly. The rain stopped and his footsteps echoed through the deserted streets. As he ran, he sometimes howled, sometimes shouted, sometimes laughed, although he was fearful and without joy. He met no-one.

Chapter Eight

Because he had nowhere else to go. Marcus began to make his way back towards the entrance to that sector of the silk pits where he worked. It was a long walk, but he was scarcely aware of the tiredness creeping through his body and for once he did not feel a hint of hunger. Twice he managed to get lost, for the streets looked different empty. Eventually he found himself on the edge of Cheapside.

He began to walk doggedly in the direction of Abacus Lane. As he passed Potter's Alley, he caught a movement with the corner of his eye.

Marcus jerked round and stared down the alley. He was certain he had seen someone, although he could see no-one now. 'Hello?' he called nervously. Then, more confidently, 'Hello down there in Potter's Alley!' He felt a welling of excitement. He was certain he had seen someone. Perhaps they were afraid to come out, to show themselves. After all, they must be as confused as he was.

He entered the alley and began to run towards the spot where he had seen the movement. 'Hello,' he called again, a little breathlessly. 'It's all right, I'm not going to harm thee!' As an afterthought he added, 'Marcus is my name.'

The alleyway was narrow, lined with the tiny potters' businesses that had given it its name. Many of the second-storey houses overhung the lane, leaving it gloomy even in daylight. He half tripped over a dead dog lying in the gutter and stumbled to a halt. 'Hello? Be anybody there?'

Potter's Alley led nowhere. Anyone leaving it must walk past Marcus. But if they were frightened and trying to hide, where *would* they hide? He was sure he had seen a movement. Maybe it was a child. 'Don't be frightened!' he called out. Even a child would be better company than no company at all.

The alley opened into a small, mean square at the bottom, lined on three sides by houses, with a high wall on the fourth. Was there a gate in the wall? He could not remember.

He trotted down to the square. It was empty. There was no gate in the wall and the wall was far too high to climb. Was he mistaken? Had he only thought he saw a movement? Master Trisram once remarked that a man saw just what he wanted to see. Gloom descended on him like a rain-cloud as he turned to go.

He saw it at once. A small door into one of the buildings was swinging gently on its hinges. He had missed it because of its position, half-hidden by the corner of the square.

'It's all right,' he called softly. 'I be Marcus Mustard. Nothing's going to harm thee.' He walked to the door and pushed it.

There was a spinner in the corridor inside. It was the size of a wolfhound – larger even than the one that nearly killed him. Marcus froze in shock. The front pair of the spinner's eight eyes swung towards him. They changed from pearl grey to black as they locked on to his own.

Chapter Nine

Marcus took a slow step backwards. The spinner watched him without moving. What he needed to do was take a step towards the spinner, reach forward calmly, take the handle and firmly pull the door tight closed. But he could no more move towards her than he could strangle her with bare hands.

He took another slow step backwards. When a spinner went for prey, she moved with lightning speed. Even now, this spinner was scant yards away. If she moved, he would never know what hit him.

Another step . . .

The spinner moved. One hairy foreleg reached up unhurriedly, hung in the air for a moment as if the creature was waving, then came down again with great deliberation. Two more of the eight eyes turned from pearl grey to black as she focused on him more intently. Marcus could hear his own heart thumping.

He licked his lips and took a third step. When the spinner still did not move, he broke and ran up Potter's Alley as quickly as his sturdy legs would carry him. Near the junction with Cheapside he risked glancing back. The spinner had not followed. All the same, he did not slow his pace.

He came at length to Chesterfield Market and could run no further. He placed his back against a wall and slid down into a sitting position. He closed his eyes and squatted for a long time, gasping. He felt sick with fear, but eventually his heart slowed and the nausea ebbed. He opened his eyes.

It was almost impossible to believe this was the place where just a day before he had hidden in the crowds from the pursuing guards. The signs of the busy market were all around him. The stalls were still in place, their goods intact. He could even see a few trays, like those used by the piemen, stacked neatly on one pavement.

He began painfully to push himself back on to his feet. As he did so, a chilling thought hit him with such force that he slid back down again. He had run from a spinner. How had the spinner left the silk pits?

The question gripped his chest so tightly he could scarcely breathe. Spinners were the most dangerous creatures on the face of Pradesh – swift, voracious predators, capable of taking prey many times their size and weight. In the wild, a single spinner no bigger than your thumb could kill a man. But in the wild, the largest spinner was about the size of a kitten. Only in Castle Dis did spinners grow as big as dogs and more. Only in Castle Dis were there *silk pits*.

Marcus recalled another legend, one almost as popular as the story of Lord Hawksmore and his Lady. It related how, in ancient times, a single spinner crawled up from the depths beneath the nomad fortress and presented herself at the Court of the King.

In those days, the Alizarin Emperor was Wolfgruff the Wise, a grizzled warrior who had seen much and consequently feared little. While his courtiers cowered as far away from the creature as they could, Wolfgruff boldly demanded what she wanted. The spinner told him she and her kind wished to be free of their cold, dark pits to enjoy the sunlight.

She proposed a bargain. If spinners were freed, she would pledge peace between the spinner race and humankind for ever.

Wolfgruff was intrigued by this suggestion, for the great spinners of Dis had long preferred human prey to any other. He was on the point of agreeing when one of his advisors, a man of wealth and greed named Coinsworth, reminded him that if the spinners left their pits, there would be none to spin the silk on which the prosperity of Dis depended.

Swayed by the words of Coinsworth, Wolfgruff ordered the spinner to return whence she came and when she refused, called on his guards to seize her. But the spinner was named Helgageerd and she was the greatest fighter of her kind. She killed the guards with ease, then moved with great speed and ferocity to kill every member of the Royal Court, sparing only Wolfgruff himself on account of his great wisdom. She then went into the streets and alleyways of Castle Dis and there killed one person in every ten she met. In the whole of the castle, there was no man who could stop her.

King Wolfgruff was so appalled by what had happened that he called on Simon Demonbinder, the greatest of his wizards, to make such magic as would return Helgageerd to her labyrinth and ensure neither she nor any of her kind ever emerged from it again.

Demonbinder demanded a great fortune for the magic. 'Soft cheese is hard won,' sighed King

Wolfgruff, echoing the first Alizarin Emperor Ansalom, and he opened his treasury and paid the price in gold bullion and rubies.

From that time on, all spinners in Dis were banished to the pits beneath the castle and bound with the greatest of magics to ensure they never emerged again.

Marcus knew that just like the story of Hawksmore, the story of Helgageerd was no more than a fable, but like so many fables, it pointed to a very real truth. The truth was that no King dared permit even a single spinner to roam outside the silk pits – the creatures were far too dangerous.

He stood up nervously. Was that spinner the only one to break free? There was no way to know. But one thing was certain. If the only other living creatures in Castle Dis were spinners, he needed to know how many were loose and where they might be, otherwise he could rest easy nowhere. Except possibly the silk pits where the living quarters were built to keep spinners out.

He walked away slowly. Somehow the idea of returning to the silk pits held no appeal. They would not be as he had known them. Prunebane would not be there. Molestrangler would not be there. The pink-eyed Cloydd would not be there. The pits would be as empty as the rest of Castle Dis. He forced his feet forward, one heavy pace at a time.

A flight of narrow, steep, stone steps led into the Mutton Market from Ware Street. Marcus, who had used them many times, ran down them quickly. As he emerged into the market square, his foot caught a small water pail on the bottom step. It tumbled, then rolled clattering across the open cobbles. At the far side of the square, a dark shape skittered from the shadows to disappear into the darkness of the underpass.

Marcus froze. Was it another spinner? He had caught only the movement and the barest glimpse of a shape, but he was certain it must be. He had seen no other living creature since he awoke. It seemed that he and the spinners were the only survivors of whatever catastrophe had befallen Castle Dis.

With only a fleeting impression he could not be certain, but he thought it must now be hiding in the underpass. The entrance to the silk pits was in the underpass.

Marcus hesitated. He could go on and use another entrance. There were three more in the sector that he knew of, the nearest little more than fifteen minutes walk. But if the spinners were escaping, he needed to know where they were breaking out. He could not repair the magic, but he might cut them off some other way.

Should he enter the underpass?

The thought terrified him. The spinner was in there in the darkness and a spinner's night vision was far better than any human. He did not dare walk in without a torch. The question was, did he dare walk in *with* one?

Marcus postponed that question while he searched for a torch. It did not take long to find one. The Mutton Market sold much more than mutton. There were sheepskin rugs and jerkins, ram's horn trumpets, bone ornaments and more besides. Without taking his eyes off the underpass for more than a moment, he picked up four mutton-fat torches in dipped-reed twist. It was a poor-quality torch which would not burn for long, but four of them would be enough.

Finding a tinderbox was far more difficult, but he came across one eventually, buried under a cracked wineskin on a curio stall. It was made from no part of the sheep that he could recognize, but it had been decorated with a scene of satyrs which included several leaping lambs.

Before he could decide whether or not his action was wise – or even sane – he found his feet carrying him slowly towards the arch. He no longer doubted a spinner had scurried in there. But had it followed the underpass to the other side, the gloomy opening into the equally foul Meat Street? Or had it done what he planned to do and taken the stairway down to the silk pits.

Or was it lurking in the darkness just beyond the archway, waiting to attack him?

An extraordinarily unpleasant thought occurred to Marcus Mustard. Until he reached the Mutton Market he had seen only two living creatures in the whole of Castle Dis. One was a spinner, the other was himself. If spinners were the only other things left alive in the castle, what did they feed on?

He shuddered. It was mad to walk into the underpass, but his feet refused to listen to his mind and carried him implacably towards the arch. Through it, after the first few steps, the underpass became a Stygian tunnel. It would take more than a minute for his eyes to grow accustomed to the gloom. A spinner without magical restraints could have him paralysed in a fraction of that time.

When he was still five yards away from the arch, he lit the first torch. It burned feebly in the daylight.

Were spinners afraid of fire? He had no way of knowing. But it was an interesting thought. Most creatures feared fire. Perhaps it might be possible to use his rush torch as a weapon.

With his free hand, he drew the short sword from his belt. The torch would not be the only weapon he had. But could he really drive off a spinner with steel and fire? He had no skill with a sword, not much skill in fighting of any sort, except the morning rough and tumble with his fellow 'prentices.

It was madness to enter the underpass.

Marcus licked his lips and took a step forward. He strained his eyes. This was the really dangerous time, for the torchlight did not penetrate the gloom. If he positively meant to step beneath that arch, there would be a moment when he was completely blind. It would last no more than an instant, but in that instant he was helpless if the spinner decided to attack.

If he stepped beneath the arch . . .

Marcus stepped beneath the arch. The darkness folded round him like a cloak. Every muscle of his body went rigid with fear, but the spinner did not attack. He held the mutton-fat torch high and suddenly he could see.

He could not see far. The torchlight sent flickering shadows little more than seven feet along the tunnel. But in that short distance at least, there was no spinner. Slowly, with infinite caution, he began to move forward.

He tried to move silently, holding his breath and making sure to place each foot slowly, firmly, so that his steps would not echo. In his mind's eye he kept seeing the spinner rushing towards him out of the blackness, forelegs lashing at him with their poisoned claws.

One step . . . two steps . . . five steps . . .

There was still no sign of any living thing within the tunnel. He tried to remember how far he would have to go in the underpass before he reached the stairway to the silk pits, but could not. He thought it might be twenty paces, but it could be thirty, perhaps even more.

. . . seven . . . eight . . . ni—

Marcus gasped and swung his sword reflexively. Then relief flooded through him in such a wave that he almost laughed. The black shape he had mistaken for a spinner was an abandoned leather sack lying half against a wall. It occurred to him that no-one had passed this way since the sack was dropped. There was always use for leather, even poor leather like this. He moved on, as slowly and cautiously as before.

He reached the steps down to the silk pits after fifty paces and stopped, locked in sudden indecision. His first torch had burned out and he was already halfway down his second. If he descended to the pits, there would be rushlights, but should he descend to the pits or search further to make sure the spinner was not hiding somewhere up ahead in the underpass?

With no warning at all, his torch went out. In pitch darkness he scrabbled panic-stricken for the tinderbox. The spark struck like a lightning flash, but the flame did not catch. He struck again and dropped the box.

Marcus went on to his knees and swept both hands across the filthy floor. To his relief he found the tinderbox at once. He struck it and lit his third torch with shaking hands. The mutton-fat flared, blinding him momentarily. He blinked the sparkles from his eyes and headed for the steps. If the spinner was further up the underpass, he did not care. He would be safer in the pits. At least he knew his way around.

Something touched him on the shoulder. Marcus screamed and spun, wildly swinging torch and sword. He saw a dark shape leap back in alarm. But it was not a spinner. It was Prudence Rainwater.

Chapter Ten

'I thought you must be dead, Marcus Mustard,'
Pru said.

'I thought *everybody* must be dead,' Marcus
said.

They were seated together in the familiar kitchens drinking a hot, thick soup of potatoes, carrots,
leeks and mutton. A large square of soft cheese,
high but good enough to eat, was set before him,
half-wrapped in muslin. (Pru had blushed a little
when she placed it there.) Were it not for the
soup, it might have been early morning of a
normal day.

Marcus, who had thought his appetite lost, was
voraciously hungry. He spooned soup as quickly
as was decent.

'Nay,' Pru said in answer to his last remark. 'Just
them as was above ground. The rest of us be fine.'

The spoon hung halfway to his mouth as Marcus
stared at her. 'The rest of us? You mean we're not
the only two?'

For some reason she would not meet his eye,
but her own eyes twinkled as she shook her head,
causing her hair to whip around her face. 'Nay,'
she said again. 'Your friends be here.' She looked
away and added, 'Some of them.'

'I saw no-one in the castle,' Marcus said with
wonder.

'Wouldn't neither – they be feared to go above.
But I bain't afeared of no spinner. We's all girls,
ain't we, them spinners and me, so I went on my

own. Nothing much to worry on, I reckon.' She grinned her lopsided grin. ''Sides, I found you.' She glanced at him sideways. 'Where'd you get the sword?'

'Found it,' Marcus said shortly. He felt guilty about the sword even though it looked as if its owner would not be coming back. But he had more important things on his mind. Obviously there was a lot he did not know. But one thing at a time. 'Who else is here?'

'I, for one!' It was Prunebane's voice, cheerful as ever, despite all.

Marcus swung round. Prunebane and Molestrangler were running across the kitchens to thump his back and shake his shoulder and tousle his hair. 'Where did you f-f-f-find him, Mistress Prudence?' Molestrangler asked delightedly. His voice, always hoarse, was doubly husky with emotion. 'We thought we'd s-s-s-seen the last of him.'

'And where did you find the broth?' Prunebane asked. He slid on to the bench beside Marcus, wiped a wooden bowl with his sleeve and began to ladle soup into it from the pot.

'Broth be my own making, Peter Prunebane, and well taught I was. Lots of food here now with fewer to go round.' She gave Marcus another sideways look and tossed her head prettily. 'Found *him* above, in the tunnel. He's got a sword now.'

They were all interest at once. 'A sword, Marcus? Show us.' This from Prunebane through a mouthful of mutton, like a royal command.

'Where did you get a s-s-s-sword?' Molestrangler asked, emphasizing the *you* just a little. 'B-b-b-bet you stole it.'

'Swords aplenty above,' Marcus said, not altogether truthfully. 'Lots else as well.' He hesitated.

''Cepting people.' He took another spoonful of soup. Beyond the pot he saw Cloydd shuffle in. His body was so twisted he moved like a crab.

'Come on,' Prunebane demanded. 'Show!' He tugged the sword from Marcus's belt and laid it on the table.

'It's just a *sh-sh-short* s-s-sword,' Molestrangler exclaimed, disappointed. 'If I was going to s-s-s-steal a s-s-sword, I'd steal a *long* s-s-s-sword.'

'Or a *broad* sword,' Prunebane put in.

'It's a real sword,' Marcus muttered, frowning. 'And I didn't steal it. I'm minding it for the owner.' To his annoyance, Prunebane giggled.

Cloydd reached the table and said shyly, 'It be good to see thee, Marcus Mustard.'

'And thee, Jacob Cloydd,' Marcus said. Then, because he was mindful of his debts, he added, 'I must thank you for what you done.'

'What I done, Marcus?'

'When you climbed the spinner thread.'

'Oh aye,' Cloydd said, embarrassed. He leaned forward to sniff the soup, his thin nose poked over the edge of the pot, a single drop of moisture teetering on its tip.

'What happened here?' Marcus asked. The soup was creating warmth in his stomach and he felt better now than he had all day. He looked from one blank face to another. 'Where be all the people?'

Prunebane glanced at Molestrangler, then said, 'We don't rightly know, Marcus. We thought you might tell us, you having been above and that.'

'And me!' Pru Rainwater put in sharply. 'I been above as well.' They ignored her.

Marcus finished his soup, wiped his mouth and shook his head. 'I know nothing. There's nobody

84

up there, nobody. It's like they were all gathered to the Mother and her Twins.'

'But the spinner didn't finish you, eh?' Cloydd grinned. He had filled a bowl with soup and was drinking clumsily. Brown liquid dripped from his chin to form a small pool on the table.

'Take more than a little s-s-s-spinner pup-pup-poison to finish Marcus,' Molestrangler said proudly. But the mention reminded him so that he asked, 'Old S-S-Squat cure you then? What did he use – stolen m-m-magic?'

'Leeches,' Marcus told him tightly. They all shivered.

'No matter,' said Prunebane, 'so long as it worked.'

'But what *happened*?' Marcus asked again. His adventure with that spinner seemed a lifetime away. 'Where are all the people?'

Molestrangler had succumbed to the soup now. 'We think they m-m-may be dead,' he said seriously between spoonfuls. 'You sure there's n-n-nobody at all up there? N-n-n-nobody *at all*?'

'I saw none,' said Marcus. He belched. 'Pardon.'

'It be a mystery, Marcus,' Cloydd said, his pink eyes shining. 'Them as went to the 'Freshing never came back.'

'He's right,' Molestrangler nodded. 'Most went above for the parade. We was all at d-d-double shift.' He grinned. ''Cause of you. We was sh-short-handed, see, you being with the Master S-S-Squat, p-p-p-pretending to be p-poisoned.'

'And lucky we were,' Prunebane said seriously. 'The other boys went up and the Masters went up and none came back.'

'Bracket's gone!' Cloydd said eagerly. They

all loathed Bracket, but Cloydd especially since Bracket liked to tease him about his red eyes and his twisted spine. He blinked. 'I'll miss Blockstump, though.'

'Blockstump's gone?' Marcus said.

'They're *all* gone,' Molestrangler said with emphasis. 'All the Masters, all the lads. We thought s-s-something must have happened up above. Like lightning—'

'Lightning?' Marcus echoed with contempt. 'Eight million people in the castle struck by lightning in the night?'

'Well, s-s-something,' Molestrangler shrugged irritably. 'I wasn't there, was I? Anyroads, we thought it was something up above—' He glared at Marcus. 'Like the B-B-Black Death maybe. And those below was s-s-spared.'

'Couldn't have been no disease,' Marcus said. 'No corpses above.'

'Couldn't have been anything special to above,' Pru said sensibly, 'since you was there and now you're here.'

'I wasn't up above last night,' Marcus told her. 'Not at the time of the 'Freshing.'

'Bain't you with Master Squat?' Pru asked.

Marcus shook his head. 'I were in the Wizards' Jail.'

It took him several minutes to get out of that one, for they insisted on hearing what had happened; then, more forcefully, what it was like inside the Wizard's Guildhall. But eventually the talk circled back.

'So you was underground as well,' said Prunebane thoughtfully. 'So we was right. Them as stayed underground was safe. Them as was above is disappeared.'

'Are we the only ones left?' Marcus asked. He looked around. 'We four?'

'Five,' said Pru.

'We five,' Marcus corrected himself. 'Are we all there is?'

'May be some left in the other galleries,' Pru suggested. She looked thoughtful. 'Difficult to know.' She was talking about the workstations scattered throughout the silk pits. But the pits themselves were a labyrinthine warren that extended under much of Castle Dis. It could take months to investigate them all.

'But we here are all we can rely on?' Marcus insisted.

'Prunebane nodded. 'Aye.'

They fell silent for a while, thinking. Then Marcus said, 'I saw a spinner up above.' To his surprise, Pru started laughing. 'What be the matter with you, then?' he asked, irritated.

'Oh, they knows about the spinners up above,' Pru said. 'They knows all about them. They wouldn't go up, not one of them. Had to leave it to a *girl* to go up.'

'It wasn't that at all,' Molestrangler said huffily, but did not explain how it really was.

'That's what they say now!' Pru crowed. 'Weren't what they said then.'

Prunebane said, 'The spinners are all over the place, Marcus. Nothing to hold them in now.'

Marcus stared at him. 'All over the place?'

'They're out of the pits,' Prunebane said seriously. 'Cloydd saw three on the west stairs going—'

'Four,' Cloydd interrupted.

'Four, was it? Cloydd saw four on the west—'

'And three more on the south,' Cloydd said. He

scraped the ladle in the bottom of the pot, then lifted the pot to pour the last of the soup.

'Anyway, a *lot* of spinners,' Prunebane said. 'Spinners survived, same as we did, and they're in the castle above now, not just in the silk pits.'

'I only saw one,' Marcus said.

'More than one up there,' Molestrangler put in. 'A *lot* more.'

'When Jacob saw them climbing up, none would leave this station,' Pru Rainwater said smugly. She raised her head, the better to look down on them. 'Excepting me. I went above, spinners or no. You saw me there, Marcus.'

'Aye, I did,' Marcus confirmed. Although he didn't know many girls very well, he'd always believed them to be weedy. Pru seemed a lot different, though. She'd certainly shown more courage than the boys when she went above; and she seemed to have a good head on her shoulders as well. But he really wanted to find out more about the spinners. 'How was it they broke out?'

'What's to stop them?' Prunebane asked with the air of one talking to an idiot.

'Magic's to stop them,' Marcus said, 'same as always.' He looked bewildered.

Cloydd gave a high-pitched giggle. 'Magic don't work no more!'

There was a new silence. Eventually Marcus said, 'What's Jacob saying?'

'Look,' Molestrangler said. He reached out and took Marcus's hand, then tugged to make him stand. Then he half dragged him out of the kitchens and on to the nearest section of the catwalk.

'What?' Marcus asked, wondering what he was supposed to be seeing.

'The globes,' Molestrangler said.

Marcus looked at the glowglobes which would normally have lit this place. They were dead as pigskins. Now it was called to his attention, he noticed that the only illumination came from a few rushlights. He assumed his friends had put them there.

'Glowglobes don't work – not here, not nowhere,' Molestrangler told him. 'Be you carrying your s-s-spellbell?'

'Mine's broke,' Marcus said. 'That's why the spinner got me.'

'Mine ain't,' Molestrangler said. 'Leastways, it weren't yesterday.' He dragged the little bell from his pocket. 'Now look.' He swung the bell violently. No sound emerged.

'It didn't chime,' Marcus said unnecessarily.

'None do,' Molestrangler said. 'Mine don't, Cloydd's don't, P-P-P-Prunebane's don't. Yours wouldn't, if it wasn't b-b-broke. Glowglobes don't work, s-s-s-spellbells don't work. P-P-Pru says the thing to take away the kitchen smells don't work now. And the spinners walk where they want. We think magic *itself* don't work no more.'

'But if magic don't work—' Marcus began; and trailed off. He looked around nervously. 'Be you saying spinners could get on this catwalk?'

'Could,' Molestrangler confirmed. 'B-b-but they like to keep clear of the light when they can.'

Which was true, Marcus thought. Spinners always preferred dark corners. The ones he had seen were both in shadows.

'That's why we p-put the rushlights out,' Molestrangler said. All the same, the talk of spinners seemed to have leeched his confidence. They walked back to the kitchens.

'See?' Cloydd called to them. 'See?'

They sat down again, ranged around the scrubbed pine table. Eventually Prudence asked, 'What be the plan now?' They all looked at Marcus.

Marcus blinked. 'Why are you asking me? I bain't got no plan – I bain't your leader.'

'Somebody'd better be,' Pru sniffed. 'Else none of us will see the next Refreshing.'

They were still looking at him – Prunebane sharp-featured, lightly built; Molestrangler much like Marcus in his build, but brown-haired and with a wide mouth full of teeth; little Cloydd, his pink eyes wide; Prudence Rainwater, who seemed older now than Marcus had remembered – and a little prettier. What she said made sense.

'I bain't your leader,' Marcus insisted, 'but should you ask, I think we need a safe place – safe from spinners.'

'What's wrong with here?' Molestrangler asked.

'Lots of food,' Pru said. 'Leastways, till it rots.'

'Nothing wrong with here,' Marcus agreed. 'Spinners don't know how to open doors. Only we'll want to go out.'

'Above?' asked Prunebane in alarm.

'Pru's right,' Marcus said. 'Lots of food now, but it will have gone off in a month. 'Sides, we can't live underground for ever. Not healthy.' He looked at Molestrangler. 'We need to make sure we got a way up that's safe from the spinners. Only thing keeping them off the catwalk now is a few rushlights.'

'Could seal the tunnel off with capture nets,' Prunebane suggested. 'Spinners can't get past a capture net.'

'Capture nets are magic,' Marcus said.

'No they bain't!' Cloydd said promptly.

'I thought they was.'

'Bain't got no magic in them,' Cloydd insisted confidently.

'Then we can use them,' Marcus said. 'That was a good idea, Peter Prunebane.'

'Nets won't keep the s-s-s-spinners off us up above,' Molestrangler muttered.

But Marcus was already climbing to his feet. 'Spinners aren't so bad up above, Raymond. I seen one, maybe two and they didn't eat me.'

The capture nets proved an excellent suggestion. There were dozens of them in the store and even the largest of them was light enough for two people to carry. The lads, who had been climbing all their working lives, found no difficulty in hanging them. Pru Rainwater, with far less experience in climbing, insisted on helping and proved to have a sure foot and a good head for heights.

Because there was a long stretch of catwalk to be covered, the operation took most of the day. When they were finished, Pru fed them again on cold roast beef, apples and several varieties of cheese. It was a novelty to eat well without having to fight for it and by the time he was finished, Marcus felt he could hardly move. The others looked the same and Cloydd kept yawning.

'We be safe enough now,' Marcus announced, hoping it was true. 'I says we washes, then sleeps. Then tomorrow . . .' He trailed off. He had no idea what they should do tomorrow.

'Don't have to wash, Marcus,' Cloydd said delightedly. 'Masters bain't here!'

'No they're not,' Marcus agreed. He grinned.

'You're right, Jacob Cloydd – we don't have to wash.'

'Where be we sleeping?' Pru asked.

'Lads sleep where we always sleep,' Marcus said. 'In the 'prentice quarters. You sleeps with the women, like always.'

'Bain't no other women now,' Pru said quietly.

Marcus stared at her. Finally he said, 'Can't sleep with us, Pru – wouldn't be right.'

'Why not?'

'You're a *girl*, aren't you? Girls can't sleep with lads, Pru – 'tisn't *right*.'

Her eyes flashed. 'I tell thee what's not right, Marcus Mustard! What's not right is accepting a girl's help and eating a girl's cooking, then telling her she mun sleep freezing on her own – that's what's not right. Spinners might get me.'

'Thought you weren't afeared of spinners!' Prunebane taunted.

'S-s-spinners can't get at us, anyroad,' Molestrangler said. 'Not here, not on the catwalk since we netted.'

But Pru did not even look towards them. 'These nights be *cold*, Marcus Mustard, 'case you hadn't noticed. I bain't sleeping on my own for all the gold in Jerico.'

Marcus looked towards his companions for support. They looked back at him blandly. Eventually he said helplessly, 'Sleep where you want, Prudence Rainwater – I'm not your Master.'

They crawled unwashed and fully clothed beneath the skins in the 'prentice quarters. Prunebane, Molestrangler and Cloydd took their familiar positions around Marcus. To his intense embarrassment, Pru snuggled up against his back. But he was too tired to stay embarrassed long. Despite her presence, he felt himself drifting.

'Marcus . . .'

He struggled to open his eyes. 'What is it, Pru?'

'I thinks I might have figured where the people went,' Pru said.

Through the fog of his exhaustion, he could not make sense of her words. 'You sleep now, Pru,' he said. And slept himself.

Chapter Eleven

Marcus woke to singing so loud and insistent that he jerked upright to find its source. This time it did not fade as quickly as before and he climbed to his feet, still half dozing – part convinced that sweet-voiced women must be in the chamber.

All but two of the rushlights had burned out in the night so the room was close to darkness. He strained his eyes. The singing had a plaintive note, like lovers calling, but as always there was no single source. One moment it seemed to be above him, the next it was below, the next all around, so that he was enfolded in the song.

He stepped carefully over Pru – on her back now, still fast asleep and snoring – then over Prunebane, and lit a rope torch from one of the remaining rushlights. He could still hear the song, sweet and clear and pure, winding through the air like a tapestry thread. He held the torch high, but there was no choir in the room, no women in the room save Pru, no persons in the room save his friends and himself, no singers to produce such song. It had a haunting, calling quality about it, like the cries of the mermaid creatures in the Mare Sirenas.

If not in the room, then outside? His torch held high, Marcus crossed the chamber and pushed through the threadbare curtain into the short corridor outside. Already the sound was fading as he wiped the sleep-sand from his eyes, and there was nothing in the corridor. He lit fresh rushlights in the corridor and kitchens then, on impulse, decided to inspect the catwalk.

By the time he had reached the heavy, banded door, the song seemed so distant he could scarcely hear it. He noticed with amusement that all bolts were firmly in place and suspected the hand of Molestrangler, who had a pessimistic streak. He drew them and opened the door.

The netting outside was alive with spinners. He had never seen so many at one time before. They crawled to form a heaving curtain. Clawed forelimbs reached towards him through the mesh. A thousand eyes glittered like black diamonds in the torchlight.

Marcus slammed the door and shot the bolts, then stood with his back against it, heart pounding. He experienced a weird mixture of relief and terror. If they had not troubled to put up the nets the night before, he would have opened the door to that nightmare of spinners. But how long could the nets keep them back? The sheer weight of the creatures must be straining the mesh already.

He closed his eyes to think. What he wanted to do was run. Run to Molestrangler and Prunebane for help. Run as far from that seething mass of spinners as he could. But did he dare take the time to run for help? The spinners might tear the nets at any second and while they could not break the banded door, they would block the only access to the world above. Without it, Marcus and his friends were trapped.

Why so many spinners? Had they sensed live food in the 'prentice quarters? He shook his head violently. Did it matter? They were *there*! Could he drive them away?

Spinners did not like light. They could tolerate

it all right – he had seen them often enough underneath the glowglobes – but they preferred dark corners. He had noticed that the rushlights Molestrangler put on the catwalk had long since burned out.

Marcus felt a sickness growing in his stomach. He knew what he should do, but he was terrified to do it. He squeezed his eyes tight, then opened them. He uttered a prayer to the Mother and Her Twins, then shot back the bolts again and opened the door.

He half expected the spinners to have broken through, but they had not. All the same, they might do at any second. He slipped through on to the catwalk and closed the door behind him. If a spinner did break through now he was trapped, but at least the others would be safe.

He tore his eyes away from the heaving mass scant yards away and set methodically to lighting fresh rushlights from his torch. He even found two new tar torches in brackets set off from the catwalk in the limestone face. They sparked and sputtered when he lit them, then flared far brighter than a score of rushlights.

Marcus glanced towards the spinners. He thought the crawling curtain might have thinned a little, but he could not be certain. Then, in desperation, he did the bravest thing of his life. He walked across the catwalk and waved his lighted torch as closely as he dared before the eyes of the nearest spinner. She stared past the torch directly at him for an instant then, to his delight, dropped off. He watched her plunge like thistledown into the pit, trailing a single cable behind her.

He backed to the door, aware that he was sweating. More spinners were dropping away now, one after another, so it seemed his plan was working. The rushlights and torches would have to be kept lit all the time. He slipped back through the door and bolted it again, more slowly this time. The full horror of their situation was at last beginning to dawn on him. They were four lads and a lass alone in a world of countless spinners. They could hide. They could be careful. If they met a single spinner they could maybe fight. But without magic, what real chance had they of surviving more than a few days?

Marcus started back to wake the others. As he passed the kitchens, Pru's voice spoke out of his memory: '*I thinks I might have figured where the people went.*' He heard his own voice answer drowsily, '*You sleep now, Pru.*'

He stuck his rope torch in a wall sconce and went to wake Pru. She was not in the 'prentice cellar, but he found her awake already in the kitchens, stirring a porridge pot. 'There then, Marcus Mustard,' she called when she saw him, 'weren't so bad sleeping with a girl now, was it? Leastways we don't make such smells as boys. You ready for porridge?'

He was ravenous after his encounter with the spinners, but he said, 'In a minute, Pru.' He perched on the edge of the table close to her and said, 'Last night, Pru, afore we fell asleep . . .'

'Aye, Marcus?'

'What you said to me, Pru – do you remember?'

'Aye, Marcus. I said I knowed where the people might be gone.'

He leaned forward. 'What was your meaning, Pru?'

She turned to smile at him, her expression a

mocking mask of innocence. 'Why, plain as your face, sir. All folks save us is gone from Castle Dis and I know where they went!' The mockery dropped from her voice. 'Leastways, I think so.' She picked up a wooden bowl and filled it with porridge from the pot. 'You eat, Marcus,' she said as she handed it to him. 'These be hard times and a man needs his food.'

Marcus sat down, flushing that she should call him a man. But he could not afford to allow his attention to wander. 'Where do you think they went, Pru?'

Prudence Rainwater sat down beside him, nursing her own porridge bowl. Although she had not washed the night before – none of them had, without Masters to drive them – she looked neat and clean this morning. He thought she might have washed her face and body while he was on the catwalk and the others were asleep.

'Nowhere,' Pru said.

Marcus stared at her.

'They didn't go nowhere,' Pru insisted. 'Not exactly. Not as what you'd call *going*.'

'You make no sense, Pru,' Marcus said gently. 'Leastways, I don't understand you.'

'They stayed,' said Pru. 'It was us as went.' She looked at him intently, as if willing him to understand. When he continued to stare at her blankly, she said, 'It were the '*Freshing*! We was due to move from Jubal Distala to Four Corms Bite.' She sniffed and ate a spoon of porridge, then leaned to look him closely in the face. 'Supposing *Castle Dis* moved from Jubal Distala to Four Corms Bite. Supposing the *castle* moved, but the people didn't!'

It hit him with the force of revelation. 'Excepting those below the ground!' he breathed.

'That's right,' said Prudence Rainwater smugly.

'Good morning, Marcus! Good morning, Prudence! What's this? Do I smell porridge? No stale ale and mouldy cheese?' It was Prunebane, who had the knack of waking lively.

'Hush, Peter,' Marcus said shortly. 'Pru's saying something important.'

Prunebane blinked, but helped himself to porridge without comment. He sat down and looked soberly at Pru. When she said nothing, Marcus muttered, 'Pru thinks it was the 'Freshing. She reckons that when the castle moved, the people didn't, 'cepting us. I think she's right.'

'How could the 'Freshing move the castle and not the people?' Prunebane asked, bewildered.

'How should I know?' Marcus glared at him. 'I'm a 'prentice wrangler, not a wizard.'

''Freshing never moved the castle on its own before.'

'Magic never broke down before,' Marcus said. It was all starting to make sense, right back to the beginning. His spellbell chimed, but the bellspell did not work the way it should. Then First Wizard Sudswarts admitted the Guild had been having problems with other spells. Now the magical corrals no longer held the spinners and not even the simplest kitchen spell would work. It looked as though magic had been running down for weeks and now it had stopped altogether.

But before it stopped, there was the 'Freshing and however much Bishop Puddifat talked about religion, the 'Freshing was pure magic, first to last. Pru had to be right. It all fitted so well. With magic running down, only the castle was moved. The people stayed. Which might mean everyone was still all right.

Molestrangler walked in, rubbing sleep from his eyes. Cloydd trailed behind him, face vacant. Both walked directly for the porridge pot without saying anything.

Marcus said, 'People aren't dead. 'Freshing left them all at Jubal Distala.'

'You can't be sure of that,' Prunebane cautioned. He looked at the other two. 'This is just an idea of Pru's.'

'Aye, and Pru's got more sense than the rest of you put together,' said Marcus with finality. He felt the rightness in his bones. He also knew now what they had to do that day. 'We got to get back to our people.'

'B-b-back?' Molestrangler frowned. He had filled a bowl with porridge and was stirring soured cream into it with some distaste. He was an ale and cheese boy in the mornings.

'To Jubal Distala,' Marcus said.

'Long way from Four Corms Bite,' Prunebane murmured. He looked up. 'We be at Four Corms Bite now after the last 'Freshing. Fourteen days by horse to Jubal Distala – near three weeks if you're drawing a wagon. You see any horses for us up above, Marcus?'

Marcus shook his head. 'Don't mean there aren't any, though.'

'S-s-s-supposing there aren't?' This from Molestrangler.

Marcus shrugged. 'Then we walk.'

'Walk?' asked Prunebane. 'That be a month or more. Where do we get the food for such a journey?'

'Food's all around you,' Marcus said patiently. 'More above ground, lots more.'

'But how shall we carry it, Marcus?'

'In a wagon,' Marcus said. 'Maybe there aren't horses, but I saw wagons enough above. Nobody to stop us taking one.'

'But if there bain't no horses, what draws the wagon?'

'We do,' Marcus said shortly.

Cloydd said, 'Supposing Pru be wrong, Marcus? I know she be smart, but just supposing. Supposing our people aren't at Jubal Distala?'

Marcus lost his temper. 'If they aren't at Jubal Distala, they aren't at Jubal Distala! What you saying we should do – stay here all alone until the spinners gets us?'

'We b-b-bain't saying that,' Molestrangler said placatingly. 'We b-b-b-bain't saying that at all. Just that it be a long walk from Four Corms B-B-Bite all the way to Jubal Distala.'

'Nobody has to walk,' Pru said. 'We hitch a wagon and we ride.'

'Marcus said he didn't see no horses up above, P-P-Pru,' Molestrangler told her. 'S-s-seems to me that when the p-p-people got left by the 'Freshing, horses might have got left as well. This is what we been saying, P-P-Pru. If there b-b-bain't no horses in the castle, where do we get horses?'

'Buy 'em,' Pru said shortly. They all turned to look at her. 'Way you all been talking, you'd think the 'Freshing left us in the middle of the Singing Desert. We be at *Four Corms Bite*! Another day or so, the first Corm trader caravan will be here. Even before that, we could walk to the nearest village in half a day and buy horses there. Bain't no problem about *horses*.'

The silence stretched until Molestrangler said almost angrily, 'Where do such as we find gold to b-b-buy a horse?'

'We got a whole castle of gold, Raymond Molestrangler. There be gold in the houses in Jerico Meadows. There be gold under the counters in the Mutton Market. We *look* for gold, that's how we find it. And if there bain't no gold, we trade goods, silk and suchlike – anything we can find.'

Marcus looked at her with admiration. She had managed to do what he had failed to do and shut up his companions. But most of all, what she said made sense. Castle Dis was now on the sacred site of Four Corms Bite, not cut off from the world. 'Pru's right,' he said decisively. 'What we need to do now is go above and search out gold or stuff to trade, like Pru says. Then I says we take it to the gates and wait till someone comes to trade. Won't be long, never is after a 'Freshing, so no sense in walking anywhere we don't have to. And think on this, lads – we're close to the gates here in the silk pits. Might have had to walk from the North Tower and that's *more* nor half a day!' His lower lip pushed out a little. 'That's what I say. Anybody say different?'

He looked from one face to another. No-one spoke. 'All right then,' he said, 'let's get us going!'

Marcus decided not to mention the spinner attack on the nets and surreptitiously made the Sign of the Twins as he opened the door to the catwalk. His luck held. Torches and rushlights were all burning brightly and there was not a spinner in sight.

Even Molestrangler settled down when they reached the surface and got clear of the gloomy tunnel. He stared around the empty Mutton Market with an expression of blank amazement. 'It's so different!'

The streets were slick with recent rain. Marcus sniffed. 'No different as ever was, except it's empty. Now, spread out and search the shops for gold.' He scratched his nose. 'Or silver – silver's not too heavy to carry. Then—'

'Or gems,' Cloydd put in, grinning. 'Gems be easy to carry too, Marcus.'

'Or gems,' Marcus agreed, although he knew there would not be many gems found in the Mutton Market. 'Anything you can get that's small, light and valuable.' A thought struck him and he asked, 'Anybody know how much a horse costs?'

They shook their heads in unison. 'Quite a lot, I expect,' Molestrangler said.

'I expect so too,' Marcus said, 'so make sure to gather plenty.' He hesitated, then added, 'Watch out for spinners.'

They regrouped in half an hour to discover that their scavenging had been successful far beyond their wildest dreams. Cloydd alone had managed seventeen gold pieces and three silver. Their combined haul seemed enough to ransom the Alizarin Emperor.

'Get a good horse or two for that,' Pru said admiringly. 'Get a whole herd of horses!'

Even Molestrangler seemed more cheerful. 'Do you want us to go to the gates now, Marcus?'

'Good a time as any,' Marcus said. Which was true enough. The formal trade caravans usually arrived on the third or fourth day following a Refreshing, but there were always tinkers and hawkers at the gates long before them. The law said you were not allowed near a sacred site within three days of the next Refreshing (in case the castle crushed you when it appeared), but nobody paid much attention when there was money to be made.

The most direct route was through Meat Street, but that meant using the dark underpass, so they skirted Bonaz Walk, cut through to Camel's Eye, then walked the whole length of Cathedral Close until they reached the south end of the Avenue of Ateliers. None of them saw a single spinner the whole while.

Eventually they reached the Courtyard of the Welcomes, a vast flagged and cobbled square that was normally a melting pot of Outlanders, sightseers and merchants. Now there was not even a guard on the huge brass gates.

'How do we open the gates, Marcus?' Cloydd asked, his eyes wide. They stood more than twenty feet high and each must have weighed tons.

'Don't have to,' Marcus told him, having been this way before. 'There be gates in the gates and doors in the gates and doors beside the gates in the pillars. Some of them got to be open.'

It proved an optimistic prediction. All outer doors and gates of Dis were closed and locked immediately before each Refreshing, and the guards had done a good job before this one. By the time they had tried five without success, Marcus was beginning to feel uneasy.

'Maybe we could break a lock,' Prunebane suggested.

'Maybe,' Marcus said tightly, though he doubted it.

'If doors won't open, maybe we should try opening the gates theyselves,' said Pru.

Marcus shook his head. 'No good, Pru. Main gates are held by magic, so they only open—' He stopped, realizing what he had just said.

All five ran back across the courtyard and stood beneath the giant gates. They looked at one another, then Pru reached out to grip the horns of an ornamental gargoyle. She tugged. The massive gate swung inwards without a sound.

'B-b-balanced nicely,' Molestrangler said admiringly.

'Come on!' Marcus exclaimed. 'We gone and wasted enough time already.' He scuttled like a spinner through the opening. And stopped. Around the castle stretched a bleak, rocky wasteland with towering cliffs on every side. They were not in Four Corms Bite. They were not at any of the Seven Sacred Sites. They were not anywhere he had ever seen.

Chapter Twelve

Three hundred yards or so from the castle walls, Marcus noticed his feet were warm. He walked a distance more, frowning, then squatted to place his palm on the shale. It was hot. He jerked his hand away and blew on his fingers.

He stood up and looked around. His friends had fanned out to explore, but Molestrangler was still in sight, as, more distantly, was Pru. 'Raymond!' he called, waving. When Molestrangler turned, he shouted, 'Feel the ground!'

Molestrangler was walking on rock. He reached down, then waved back. 'Warm!' he called.

They walked on. Marcus topped a rise and found himself looking down on a mud pool that bubbled like simmering porridge. A few yards away, a vent released a constant plume of smoke and steam. Marcus had never seen anything like it, but at least he could guess what it was. The last Refreshing must have put Castle Dis down near a volcano. What he was looking at was a thermal mud spring and fumarole.

It explained something that had been puzzling him. The weather felt too warm for spring, even late spring. Thinking back, he should have suspected they were not at Four Corms Bite. It was not just the heat: there had been too much rain as well.

He walked on, carefully skirting the mud. The cliffs were further away than they had seemed at first, but there was still no obvious break in them. He was hoping to stumble on a road, or track, although there was no sign of one so far. The whole place had a desolate feel about it, as if people had never lived here.

He glanced around and found both Pru and Molestrangler had now disappeared from view. It increased the sense of desolation. But the feeling was mixed with something else, something more personal. Marcus had spent his entire life in Castle Dis, in its dim-lit silk pits or its teeming streets. There was no law to stop him exploring the countryside around the keep (so long as he was back before the next Refreshing), but he could never afford to.

Now, for the first time, he walked in truly open countryside – or as open as the surrounding cliffs permitted – and it made him feel strange. He was nervous, excited, frightened and a little in awe, as he had once felt when he was herded with more than a score of apprentice wranglers into Bishop Puddifat's cathedral.

The shale beneath his feet gave way to black volcanic soil which grew no grass at all, but supported tiny clumps of twisted plants. Nothing reached higher than his waist and there were no trees. Curiously, he reached down and crumbled soil between his fingers. It was not so hot as the shale, but it was warm.

There was still no sign of a break in the surrounding cliffs. An unhappy suspicion was growing in Marcus's mind. On horse or on foot, he might not find a way out of this place. He hoped the others were having better luck.

The patch of soil gave way to rocks – not high, but sharp-edged and hotter, if anything, than the shale. As he scrambled up, he began to sweat and even when he stopped for breath, the rivulets continued to trickle down his forehead and along his nose. An unpleasant thought occurred to him. This place was so strange that Castle Dis might no longer be in the world of Pradesh at all. Who could tell how wrong the Refreshing had gone? The castle might have set down in a Chaos Hell. He remembered the demon creature inside the pillar in the Wizards' Guildhall and shuddered.

He reached the summit of the rocks and began, carefully, to climb down the other side. The scene below was more pleasant than the immediate surrounds of the castle. He was looking into a shallow valley with grassland and a pool fed by a narrow stream.

Marcus scrambled down. The pool looked more inviting by the minute. As he left the rocks, he realized that the grassland was not grassland at all, but a covering of lichen which felt spongy underfoot. The water of the pool smelled of sulphur, but was clear enough to let him see the pebble bottom. It deepened towards the middle, but looked safe enough. Marcus licked his lips and carefully tested the temperature with one hand. It was not just warm, but pleasantly hot, like a bath.

Marcus could not remember ever taking a hot bath. The Masters insisted their apprentices washed nightly, whether they needed to or not. But it was a cold wash with gritty soap, standing naked by the water troughs. He had heard of hot baths, of course. The aristocracy in Jerico Meadows had them in golden tubs filled by trains of servants. But he had never known anybody who had actually had one. Bathing in hot water sounded like heaven.

He glanced around. The valley was cut off from view and his friends were well out of sight. He knew he should be looking for a path, but a few minutes would not make any difference. He shrugged out of his clothes and ran into the pool.

It was bliss. The water wrapped around him like a mother's arms. By keeping near the edge, he found he could lie down without fear of drowning. He lay, half floating, as the pool soaked out pains he did not even know he had. He closed his eyes and gave himself up to one of the most wonderful experiences of his life.

Marcus's eyes opened with a jerk as he realized he had been dozing. He glanced upwards in the hope of catching the sun's position, but the sky was overcast. Still, he did not think he had dozed for long. He climbed guiltily from the pool and scurried towards his clothes.

'Marcus? Be you down there?'

He froze. It was Pru. She was standing on a rocky outcrop no more than twenty yards away. Her back was to him and she had not seen him, but she was looking along the valley and must soon turn in his direction.

Marcus grabbed his drawers and hurried to pull them on. In his haste, he managed to put both feet in one leg. He tugged and sent himself hopping wildly off balance. 'Don't look round, Pru!' he screamed desperately. 'I'm naked! Don't look round!'

Pru looked round. She grinned. 'Why be you dancing with no clothes on, Marcus Mustard?'

She watched curiously as he extricated his foot, hoisted his drawers and grabbed his breeches. He was flushing crimson as he pulled them on.

Pru joined him as he struggled into his shirt. She was carrying something in her apron. 'Look see, Marcus. Look at this.'

Marcus did up the last remaining buttons and looked. Her apron was full of clear white crystals, several of them big as hen's eggs. He stared at them, so fascinated that it wiped away his embarrassment.

'Be they diamonds?' Pru demanded eagerly.

Marcus peered closely. 'I don't think so, but they're awful pretty.'

Pru sniffed. 'Bain't diamonds, bain't much good.' She shook out her apron and the hoard of crystals scattered on the ground.

'Don't do that!' said Marcus in alarm. 'Even if they're not diamonds, maybe they're worth something.'

She shrugged. 'If they be, there be plenty more beyond the rise. Gets hundreds of them all about the rocks, you do.' She looked at him shrewdly. 'You bain't found no road, have you?'

He shook his head, flushing again.

'No more have I,' Pru said. 'Mayhap we should look together.' She took his elbow. 'That way you bain't likely to fall in no more water.'

Pru climbed rocks like a mountain goat. Marcus struggled after her, his body and clothes steaming as the heat dried him out. They searched for three-quarters of an hour without sign of track, road or human habitation. They were approaching a cliff-face.

'There be a cave up there,' Pru said, pointing. The dark entrance was less than twenty feet above their heads.

'Best keep out of caves,' Marcus said firmly, wary without knowing why.

'Might be a tunnel through,' Pru said. She had already started climbing. Marcus had no option but to follow her.

Marcus pulled himself over the lip of an external ledge as Pru disappeared into the cave. 'There be stuff in here,' she called out.

'What sort of stuff?' Marcus asked breathlessly as he stood up. He would have preferred her not to have gone in alone, or at all, but there was no talking to the girl.

'Stuff such as I don't know of.'

Frowning, Marcus walked into the cave. Pru was standing just inside the entrance, staring at a large mound of furred spheres. Each was about the size of her fist. Marcus recognized them instantly. 'Out!' he told Pru sharply.

She looked around at him in surprise. 'What be they, Marcus?'

He grabbed her wrist and glanced around the cave in growing panic. 'Spinner eggs!' This time when he tugged there was no resistance and they clambered down from the cave like frightened monkeys.

'What be we going to do now?'

'We're going back to join the others,' Marcus told her grimly. A dark suspicion was growing in his mind, but he did not want to face it.

They met up with the others by prior arrangement in the tap-room of a deserted tavern near the castle gates. The ale had turned sour and the cheese was mouldy, but there was a loaf of coarse black bread that seemed all right, a pitcher of fermented mare's milk that tasted sweet, and a whole barrel of fine green apples. The food, such as it was, had failed to lift anybody's spirits.

'I votes we get back to the silk pits,' Mole-strangler said thickly. The mare's milk had raised his colour, slurred his speech and temporarily cured his stammer.

'Well,' Marcus said, 'we shouldn't tarry here.' He wanted to get moving before it grew dark. He had a feeling there might be spinners crawling on the streets of Castle Dis after dark. But he wasn't sure he wanted to go back to the silk pits.

'What's wrong with here?' demanded little Cloydd. He had drunk more of the mare's milk than anyone and it had made him aggressive.

'Nothing wrong with here,' Prunebane said gently. 'Raymond only means we will be safer in a place we know.'

'Safer,' Cloydd echoed.

Pru said earnestly, 'Things be changed since this morning.'

Marcus said, 'We aren't at Four Corms Bite, that's for sure. 'Freshing hardly worked at all, by the looks of it. Didn't take us to the Bite, didn't take us to any sacred site I know of. Took us . . . somewhere else.' He was near terror that he knew where, but did not want to tell the others until he had time to think about it.

'Aye,' said Molestrangler. 'And by the looks of those cliffs, we bain't going back. Not on horse. Not on foot. Not anyhow.'

That was the worst of it. When they compared notes, it was obvious the castle had set down in an enormous natural crater. It was surrounded on all sides by sheer cliffs, with neither road, nor track, nor break in them. They were cut off from the outside world.

'Maybe the Emperor will send for us,' Prune-bane suggested. Clearly he meant send to find the castle, since nobody worried about four apprentice wranglers and a kitchen maid.

'Might,' Pru said. 'Then again, he might not. But if he does, won't he think the castle went to Four Corms Bite, same as us? If he sends anywhere, he'll send to Four Corms Bite and when he don't find it there, what then?'

She was looking at Marcus, but he didn't answer. He was still struggling with the conviction that he knew where they were.

'What's matter, Marcus?' Pru asked at once.

To distract her, he said, 'I don't think we can rely on the Emperor finding us. I think what we've got is what we've got and it might be a while afore it changes.'

Cloydd looked at him vacantly and blinked his strange pink eyes. 'What have we got, Marcus?'

Pru answered for him. 'We got an empty castle and we got spinners and we got usselves. That's all we got, Jacob Cloydd.'

'That's all,' said Marcus soberly. 'And if we aren't to be food for spinners, we better find us a safe place for the night.' He had a feeling that particular problem might be more urgent than any of them imagined.

'That's what I be saying!' Molestrangler exclaimed. 'We needs to get b-back to the silk pits.'

But Pru shook her head. 'I bain't rightly sure of that, Raymond. Now the magic's gone, there's spinners in the castle, that's for sure. But there's more in the pits. And them as left the pits is still *near* the pits. I knows why you wants to go back, Raymond. We five of us has lived below and we knows the station and it feels safe. But think on this: how safe is it now the magic's gone?'

Marcus looked at them, wondering if he should tell them his suspicions. He wished they could have seen what he had seen that morning, with the spinners crawling over the nets they had hung for their protection.

'Maybe so, m-m-maybe not,' Molestrangler muttered uncertainly.

'One thing more,' Prunebane said. 'Only way we can get into the station now is through the underpass. How long before spinners move into that tunnel?'

'You got something there,' Molestrangler said at once. He bit down on his fourth apple. 'All right, where do you say we go?'

Although he hadn't really thought about it, Marcus heard himself say, 'South Tower.'

'Why South Tower, Marcus?' Prunebane asked.

South Tower was an ancient quarter of the castle, but the tower itself had been rebuilt from the ground up just five years before. Because it was near the Great Gates where the merchants and the pilgrims entered after each Refreshing, it had been faced with crystal quartz and mica as a landmark. When there was so much as a single ray of sunshine, it glittered like a beacon.

'There be food stores there,' Marcus said. Like all the towers, the South Tower was home to a regiment of the Alizarin guards. He had never been there, but it made sense to suppose there must be stores. Men had to eat.

'Food's important,' Pru said. 'Soft cheese be hard won.'

'B-better food nor what we're used to, I'll warrant,' Molestrangler mused thoughtfully. 'Guards get best of everything.'

'Second,' Marcus said, encouraged by the

response, 'we'll be near the Great Gates, so if anything does come, we sees it coming.' He realized at once he had said too much, but they did not seem to notice. They were nodding, so he carried on quickly: 'By the same token, we'll be close to the gates for getting out if the castle moves again.'

'How can the castle move again without a 'Freshing?' Prunebane asked. 'Won't be no more 'Freshings if magic's gone.'

He was right, but Marcus ignored him. 'Third, any guard quarters is always built sound against attack. We gets in there and shuts the doors and there bain't a spinner can get near us.'

'What b-b-be we waiting for?' Molestrangler asked dramatically.

They could see the South Tower from the tavern, but it took almost two hours to reach it – mainly because Prunebane insisted he knew the way and proved he did not. 'There,' he said annoyingly as they walked through the arch into the surrounding plaza, 'I knew it be around here someplace.'

Marcus drew in his breath sharply and stopped so suddenly that Cloydd bumped into him. It was not just the South Tower that had been rebuilt, but the whole of the South Plaza. An hypnotic spiral mosaic, inlaid in glass and marble on the plaza floor, led the eye towards the monumental statue of Leon Dark, the Alizarin Emperor.

Lord Dark was carved from a vast block of obsidian, creating a figure that punned his name. But what held the eyes, what riveted the attention, were the sheets of colour and lightning flashes which played sinuously and continuously around the entire sculpture.

'Magic bain't all gone!' breathed Pru, echoing his own thought. She was standing by his shoulder, wide-eyed.

'Bain't magic,' Prunebane said beside them.

'Lights be magic,' Pru said.

Prunebane shook his head. 'Lights be something they call 'lectricity. Weren't no wizard set them going.'

'What be it then?'

Prunebane shrugged. 'Something a woman contrived with fur and amber, so they say. 'Lectricity, they calls it. Bain't much use for anything, but it be pretty.'

Beyond the statue soared the South Tower, its crystalline quartz facing glittering. A red tinge in the evening sun was beginning to turn it into a pillar of fire. The doors, once held by magic locks, were lying open. To Marcus's great relief, there were stout bolts on the inside.

The tower proved everything he had hoped. Its walls were nearly eight feet thick, its doors four inches of fine oak. There were bars on each slit window. The place was a fortress; and, if he was right, exactly what they would need. Behind the defences were living quarters, sleeping quarters and kitchens so luxurious that the others talked of nothing else – at least, until they found the food stores which extended through thirteen basement rooms. If need be, they could stay inside the tower for months and not go hungry.

That night when the others had gone to sleep off the enormous stew Pru cooked them, Marcus noticed his hand was shaking. He watched it with interest. The tremors came regularly, about fifteen seconds apart. Every third tremor was so strong it

116

shook the table. He did not know what to do. He was certain he knew where the castle was now and if he was right, they were doomed.

'Marcus . . . ?'

He glanced round. 'Hello, Pru.' He slid his hand casually below the table and sat on it to steady it.

'Bain't thee want to sleep this night?'

'I'm coming in a minute, Pru.' He smiled at her weakly.

'None of us be worth a candle if we don't take time to sleep.'

'I know that, Pru. I'm coming, really. In a minute.'

'See to it that you do, Marcus Mustard.' She hesitated, then added softly, 'I be lonely without you.'

'Pru, I—' Marcus began, but it was too late. She had slipped from the kitchen to return to bed. He stared after her. He should have been pleased – a part of him *was* pleased – but he could think of nothing for long except the spinners.

They were all afraid of spinners, but none of them suspected how bad it was about to get. The spinners liked live food. He held his head in his hands, eyes closed against the nightmare. Every fifteen seconds or so, he felt the tremor.

'Marcus . . . ?' He looked up. Pru had come back again. 'What's the matter, Marcus?'

Of a rush, he decided to tell her. 'I know where we are, Pru.'

She sat down on the bench beside him and slid her arm around his shoulders. 'Where be we, my Marcus?'

He looked at her with desolation in his eyes. 'We be in the Pooka Ginid.' He knew she did not understand. She had probably never heard of Scrof the Younger or how he found the Land of Sprites and Spirits. He had only learned the story himself because it was taught to wranglers. Why should he expect Pru to know the castle now sat in the middle of the spinners' ancient breeding ground? Why should he expect Pru to know this was the hatching season and within days the land – and Castle Dis – would crawl with spinners by the million?

Chapter Thirteen

Marcus woke to silence. There was neither singing nor the sounds of his companions sleeping. For a moment he lay still, fearful but not remembering why. For a moment he did not know where he was.

He looked around. The dormitory was far from the 'prentice cellar. It occupied the turret room of the South Tower. The floor was covered with rush matting of a type Marcus had never seen before. The weave seemed plain enough, but something subtle in its making gave it a pattern in the morning light.

Marcus remembered the root of his fear.

He was alone in the dormitory. He had come to bed late, slept late and now the others were awake and up before him. Once on such a morning he would have worried on missing the soft cheese. Now it didn't matter.

He sat up and swung his feet from the bunk, marvelling at the warmth of the matting. He pulled on new breeches over his new drawers, both found in the stores Prunebane had discovered. The breeches were a little loose, but clean, unpatched and warm. They were softer than any garment he could ever remember.

Marcus went to the slit window and looked out. The plaza below was empty, as were the surrounding streets. He offered a prayer to the Mother and Her Twins. There was still no sign of the hatchling swarm.

He returned to his bunk and finished dressing, then left the dormitory and took the spiral staircase to the lower floors. As expected, he found his four friends in the kitchens. They stared at him as he entered. He knew at once that they knew. He nodded wearily at Pru Rainwater. 'You told them.'

Pru nodded back. 'Just now, Marcus Mustard.'

'B-b-be you certain this be the P-P-Pooka ah-Ginid, Marcus?' Molestrangler asked anxiously, his head twisting on the *Ginid*. He blinked, then looked at Marcus with wide eyes.

'I'm not certain,' Marcus said truthfully, 'but I'm nearly certain.' He looked at the table. It was laid to a weird selection of dried fish, black bananas, and seven loaves of grainy bread. There was nothing to drink except what looked like a pitcher of freeze-distilled brandy, which no-one dared touch in the morning and hope to remain upright through the day.

'Pru says we mun all takes turns at getting breakfast,' Prunebane muttered apologetically. 'It were my turn today.'

Marcus sat down heavily. There was no appetite in him. 'You remember they learned us how the spinners came to Dis,' he told Molestrangler. 'You remember Scrof the Younger? We used to laugh because his name sounded like a disease.'

Molestrangler nodded grimly. 'Aye.'

'Think on the story,' Marcus said. 'Here be high cliffs. Here be crystals. Here be twisted plants. Here be heat. Here be spinner eggs. Isn't that the Pooka Ginid?'

'I found crystals, for sure,' said Pru.

'Weren't s-s-so many s-s-s-spinner eggs you found,' Molestrangler said. 'S-s-s-supposed to be caves-full in the ah-Poh ah-Poh ah-Pooka nga-Ginid.' His stammer was floating from one set of words to another, as it did when he was particularly upset.

'I found more in a cave,' said Prunebane.

'You didn't tell us!' Molestrangler snapped accusingly. Prunebane said nothing.

Marcus took a deep breath. 'If this is the Pooka Ginid in truth, we must expect the hatchling swarm.'

'What be the hatchling swarm, Marcus?' Cloydd asked. He had been a 'prentice for just four years, and so had missed the last one.

Marcus said, 'Spinners' eggs come out in spring, all at the same time. None knows why.'

'Every five years,' Prunebane put in.

'Every five years in the silk pits,' Marcus corrected him. 'But that be because it be held that way by magic—' (When magic worked, he thought.) 'In nature, the swarm comes every year. The hatchlings be little, compared to spinners, but even in the pits they comes out in thousands. A place like this, the Pooka Ginid, they must come out in millions.' He wondered how dried fish would taste first thing in the morning. He looked from face to face. 'When they come out, they're so hungry they eat each other, which cuts down the numbers. But afore they do that, they eat anything else living.'

After a long moment, Pru said, 'Marcus . . .?'

He turned towards her.

'You said in the pits that the Masters hold back the swarm by magic?'

'That's right, Pru.'

'Magic don't work no more,' Pru said. 'Do that mean a little swarm from the pits as well as a big swarm from the Pooka Ginid?'

Marcus rubbed his eyes. 'I don't know, Pru. I think so.'

'And before they eat each other, they be going to try to eat us?'

He said nothing.

Cloydd, who was actually nibbling on the dried fish, said, 'When will the swarm come, Marcus?'

Marcus shrugged. 'I don't know exactly. Maybe tomorrow or the day after.' Then, because he was an honest lad, he added, 'Maybe today.'

'But we be all right here, Marcus?' Cloydd asked anxiously. 'I mean, we be safe here, in the tower?'

Marcus said brutally, 'We be safe from grown spinners, that's for sure, but hatchlings get in everywhere, lessen you hold them back by magic. There be no magic anywhere as Pru says, let alone here.'

'What's to do, Marcus?' Prunebane asked.

Marcus said, 'I don't know.'

'C-c-can't we ah-m-m-make the t-t-tower p-p-proof against the hatchlings?' Molestrangler asked.

'I don't think so,' Marcus said. 'You seen hatchlings yourself. Some be no bigger than your fingernail.'

'And all be poison,' Prunebane said gloomily.

'Are we going to die then?' Cloydd asked anxiously.

To Marcus's surprise, it was Pru who answered firmly. 'Bain't going to die if we can help it, Jacob. Maybe we can't seal the whole tower, but we mun try to seal a room. We fills it with food and we stays there and we waits. Hatchling swarm can't last forever, not if they eats each other like Marcus says.'

It was true. The worst of the swarm was usually

over in three days. Marcus cheered up a little, but only a little.

'What's matter, Marcus?' Pru asked.

'Nothing's matter, Pru. That's a good idea. A very good idea and we must try it. Only . . .'

'Only what?' Molestrangler asked.

'Only after the swarm, there's still an awful lot of spinners. Little ones stay little for a month or more—' He caught Pru's expression and said quickly, 'I know we could stay inside for that time, I know that. But we got to come out sometime and when we does, the spinners will be waiting.'

'Then,' said Pru reasonably, 'we mun get out before they come.'

'No way through the cliffs,' said Marcus gloomily.

'I f-f-found a way,' Molestrangler said. When the heads swung towards him, he added sheepishly, 'I found it yesterday.'

Prunebane stared at him in amazement. 'You didn't say!'

'I didn't s-s-s-say because it be d-d-dangerous.'

'Bain't no more dangerous than staying here!' Pru said angrily.

'Do you really know a way, Raymond?' Marcus asked.

Molestrangler nodded. He looked angry, as he often did when he badly needed to talk and his stammer was in full swing. 'B-b-bain't no good for horses, even if we had them, ah-b-ah-but I thinks we might get out on foot, iffen we climb.'

'Difficult climb?' Marcus asked cautiously.

Molestrangler said seriously, 'We be 'prentices, b-b-bain't we?' He meant that apprentice wranglers spent their lives on spinner webs. They were all expert climbers.

'Pru's no 'prentice,' Marcus said.

'I can still climb,' Pru snapped back quickly.

Molestrangler said nothing. Marcus stood up. 'Maybe we should look at this place you found, Raymond. Will you show us?'

It was raining lightly by the time they reached Molestrangler's cliff-face. The water on the warm rocks created a sodden mist that rose to meet the rain. All five dripped as if they had jumped into a stream.

'Where's the path?' Prunebane asked.

'B-b-bain't no path,' Molestrangler said, pointing. 'Look there.'

Marcus swept his eyes upwards, but could see nothing but cave-mouths. The cliff seemed to be honeycombed with them. He thought of hatchlings pouring from them in a constant stream and felt his stomach chill.

Prunebane's eyes were sharper. 'The ledge, Raymond? You mean the ledge?'

'Aye,' Molestrangler said. 'Don't you think it winds all way up to the top?'

Marcus saw the ledge now. It was narrow and two different sections seemed to have crumbled away, but he followed it with his eyes and thought Molestrangler might be right.

'I think it does,' Prunebane confirmed hesitantly. 'By the Mother and Her Twins, Raymond, you might be right!'

Marcus said, 'You think any of us could climb that, Raymond?' He was looking at one of the crumbled sections.

'Mayhap we have to,' Molestrangler said.

'I'm not sure any of us could climb there,' Marcus said uncertainly.

Cloydd, who had been silent as a church mouse

since they left the castle, said suddenly, 'Some on us might. I might.' Which was true enough. Cloydd was the best climber among them.

'Aye,' Marcus said, 'but that's not much good to those of us as can't.'

Prunebane looked up with narrowed eyes, studying the ledge. 'What say one goes and brings back help? The rest on us stays.'

Marcus frowned at his feet. He had no idea how far they were away from help, or how rough the going might be in between, but if Prunebane's idea was not perfect, he could not think of any other. 'Which on us should go?' he asked.

'The b-b-best climber,' Molestrangler said promptly.

'Jacob Cloydd be the best climber,' Prunebane pointed out. Which was true, but Cloydd was also simple. They dared not trust him to get help.

'Yes, I be,' said Cloydd proudly.

Marcus found his eyes attracted to the caves. Hatching could occur at any time. They were risking their lives this close to the swarm. 'We better decide soon. Somebody better get started.'

'Can't go till tomorrow,' Molestrangler said. 'I b-b-bin up there. There be a—'

'You been up there?' Prunebane squealed. 'You never told us you been up there!'

Molestrangler ignored him. 'There be a cross wind comes up. B-b-blow you clean off if you try to n-go too far.'

'Then we can't get out that way.' This from Marcus, irritation in his voice.

'Early morning, f-f-first thing. B-b-before the w-w-wind gets up.' Molestrangler smiled suddenly.

They trooped back to the South Tower and selected a room to seal against the hatchling swarm when it arrived. As they began to haul in food and other necessities, they argued about who should go. Oddly enough, it was Cloydd who solved the dilemma. 'Why bain't we drawing straws?' he asked.

Pru found the straws in an old mattress. She laid out five on a small table then fished scissors from her apron to shorten one.

'That be five straws,' Marcus said.

'There be five of us, Marcus Mustard,' Pru told him quietly.

'No sense you drawing a straw, Pru,' Prunebane said.

'Why would that be, Peter?' Prudence asked him sweetly.

For some reason he missed the danger signs. ''Cause you be a *girl*, bain't you? Can't let you risk a climb like that.'

'You planning to stop me, Peter Prunebane?' Pru asked with such venom that Prunebane actually fell back a step.

'If Pru wants to draw straws, I think we should let her,' Marcus put in hurriedly. It was partly to keep the peace, but partly because he had revised a lot of his opinions about girls since he had got to know Pru.

'But Pru can't climb as well as we can!' Prunebane protested.

'Pru can climb well enough,' said Marcus bluntly. He was remembering how they'd clambered over rocks together and investigated the cave with the spinner eggs. There had been times when her agility had left him breathless.

'I dunno . . .' Prunebane said uncertainly. He glanced around the others in search of support, but they avoided his eye.

126

'Are we all agreed on what we're doing?' Marcus asked to defuse the situation.

'We be drawing straws to see who climbs,' said Pru firmly. She too looked around and no-one contradicted her.

'Aye,' Marcus said, 'and whoever climbs must go quick for help and bring it here to rescue those who stayed behind. Agreed?'

'Agreed!' they nodded.

'He as goes must take food,' Marcus said. 'We mustn't forget that.' He caught Pru's eye. 'Or she as goes,' he added as a sudden afterthought.

'Food,' Cloydd echoed. He had been carrying dried beef strips into their chosen room.

'And a weapon,' Marcus said. 'In case.'

'Your sword,' said Molestrangler promptly.

Marcus nodded. 'Just so. Whoever goes must take my sword.' He looked around. 'Now supposing he – they falls?'

'Supposing they does?' Prunebane asked.

'I say we watch from the turret,' Marcus suggested. 'Should be able to see from there. If they falls, somebody else must go at once and try the climb.'

'What happens if both falls, Marcus?' Cloydd asked. He grinned widely.

'We worry about that then,' Marcus told him. 'Are we all agreed so far?'

They looked at one another uncertainly and mumbled, 'Yes.'

'Now,' Marcus said briskly, 'how shall they find help, the one who climbs?'

There was a long, dull pause. Then Pru said suddenly, 'Whoever climbs, climbs again. When they gets beyond the cliffs, they climbs a high place and looks around. If they can see sign of people, they goes that way. If they don't, they walks south an hour then climbs the next high place and looks around. Keep doing that and they be bound to see something sometime.'

It sounded as good a way as any. Wondering if he might have forgotten something, Marcus said, 'Let's draw the straws.' If Cloydd drew the short straw, they would have to draw again, but he would worry about that if it happened. Just as he'd worry about what would happen if Pru drew the short straw.

'I be one to hold the straws,' Pru announced, 'but Cloydd should mix them up since I cut them so I don't know which be short.' She turned her back on the table. Cloydd scuttled forward and shuffled the straws, grinning broadly. He looked as if he was playing a game. When he had finished, Pru reached behind her and picked them up. As Cloydd returned to his place, she rolled them between her palms to mix them further. Then she walked to the middle of the room, her right hand clasped before her. Five straws protruded from it.

'You first, Jacob, seeing as you be the best climber.'

Cloydd reached for a straw, hesitated, touched one, drew back, gripped another, then let go of it to select the first he had touched. The straw he drew seemed long as it slipped through Pru's fingers, although it was difficult to say for sure. Cloydd smiled broadly at everyone in the room.

'Now me,' said Pru, 'seeing as I be the worst.' She shot a mischievous glance at Prunebane and drew a straw with her left hand.

She walked to Molestrangler. 'Now you, Raymond, because you found the way out.'

'M-m-m-m-maybe!' Molestrangler said explosively. He saw the blank expression on Pru's face and added, 'M-m-maybe a w-w-way out. You never know.' He took a straw.

She went to Prunebane. 'Now you, Peter Prunebane.'

'Thank you, Pru,' said Prunebane. He hesitated, then said, 'I be sorry I made you cross.'

She ignored him and came to Marcus, the last straw slightly bent between her fingers. 'Bain't much option for you, Marcus Mustard.'

Marcus reached for the final straw and drew it from her hand. It looked exactly the same length as the others and they looked the same length as each other. Prunebane must have noticed too, for he said, 'You forgot to cut one short, Pru.'

'Not I,' said Pru decisively. 'But I made it just a little short, so no-one could cheat. We mun measure the straws 'gin one another.' She raised her voice. 'But before you do . . .'

They had been walking towards one another. They stopped.

'. . . but before you do,' Pru repeated, 'don't forget whoever makes the climb be climbing for us all. They mun come back with help and come back quick, else them as stays behind . . .' She let it trail off. They all knew those who stayed behind would die.

They laid their straws on the small table and smoothed them out. Pru was right. One straw was a little shorter than the rest. It belonged to Marcus Mustard.

Chapter Fourteen

He heard singing, the strangest yet. In place of the choir, there was one voice – a pure, sweet soprano which swooped and climbed like a bird in flight. Through this wordless song, one word eventually emerged . . . or so he thought. As he lay dozing in the warmth and comfort of his bunk, the singing voice called, *Marcus . . . Marcus . . . Marcus . . . Marcus . . .*

Marcus swam up to wakefulness and listened to the singing fade. The others were asleep in their bunks, innocent of the grey dawn light that wakened him. He swung his feet to the floor and went to the window. Streets and plaza were still empty. The hatchling swarm had not yet begun.

He walked back to his bed and dressed. He wasn't hungry, but he went quietly down the spiral staircase and forced himself to eat the spiced meat and pickle Pru had left out for him the night before. He would carry food with him, of course, but when he reached the top – *if* he reached the top – he had no idea how long it would have to last. Best to start on a full stomach.

He stacked the food pack beside the outer door, then climbed the spiral stairway back up to the turret room to wake the others. They came to slowly, staring up at him with disbelieving eyes.

'Get from thy beds,' said Marcus cheerily. 'I'm off now to find some help for you.' When he was sure they were fully awake, he added more soberly. 'Watch me from the turret here. If – when

I reach the top, go to the room we chose and seal it. The swarm hasn't started yet, but that don't mean it won't; and soon. Stay inside, don't go out for any reason and believe I shall return with help.' It came to him that if he could find a wizard, the wizard might know what had happened to the magic – maybe even make it work again. He couldn't think of any way to control a mass of spinners that did not involve magic.

Still in her bunk, Pru said, 'Marcus, I mun ask you something.' She crooked her finger until he bent over her, then whispered, 'Will you kiss me farewell, Marcus Mustard?'

Marcus flushed more deeply than the time when she had seen him naked. He glanced at his friends in the remaining bunks. Cloydd seemed to have slipped back into sleep, but Prunebane and Molestrangler were watching him with interest. He looked back at Pru, opened his mouth to refuse, then kissed her briefly instead.

'Oooooh!' chorused Molestrangler and Prune-bane in unison. Pru grinned at him delightedly.

They waved him goodbye at the main entrance door of the tower and he was doubly embarrassed when Pru wept. He left quickly, the food pack strapped to his back and the short sword stuck in his belt. He felt worried about the sword, which would be awkward in a climb, but felt worst about leaving it behind. Reaching the cliff-top was only the first of his problems. Reaching help could involve several days journeying and who knew what he might meet on the way.

As he left the castle gates, an odd feeling of relief swept over him. The hatchling swarm might start at any second, he might fall to his death while climbing the cliff, he might lose his way while trying to find help. He might, for all he knew, be eaten by a dragon, but at least he was doing something. Only now did he realize how heavily inaction had been weighing on him.

In twenty minutes, Marcus reached the cliff-face. He stared upwards, studiously ignoring the cave-mouths from which the hatchlings would emerge. If the swarm began while he was standing here, he would die. If the swarm began while he was climbing, he would die. Even if the swarm began after he had reached the top, he might die if he was not well clear – it depended on how far the breeding grounds extended. But there was nothing he could do about any of it.

The ledge Molestrangler had found began about twenty-five to thirty feet above him, but there were enough handholds and footholds to give him confidence that he could reach it. He shifted his backpack, adjusted the awkward sword and swung himself up on to the cliff-face.

It was hard going. Like most 'prentices he had a good head for heights, but when he climbed in the silk pits, he climbed on the webs. Web-walking was a special technique, not at all like cliff-climbing. Long before he reached the ledge, his hands were bleeding and his arms ached. His worry about the sword proved unfounded – he scarcely noticed it at all during the climb – but his food pack grew heavier by the minute and seemed intent on pulling him outwards.

Marcus rested, clinging to the cliff-face like a spinner. He kept thinking of Pru, who had wanted him to kiss her, and of their small, brief kiss. He had never kissed a girl before.

He reached for another handhold and climbed on. After a few more minutes, he noticed the cross-wind Molestrangler had mentioned. It was not yet strong, but it chilled his body. At first the effect was pleasant, after the sweating volcanic heat below, but after a while his hands numbed so that he was less sure of his grip. He began to wonder if his climb would fail even before he reached the ledge.

But reach it he did; and without serious problems. He swung his legs over and collapsed face down, panting. His arms were sore and trembling with the strain, but at least now he had an easy time ahead until he reached the parts where the ledge had crumbled.

He rested until his heartbeat slowed, then climbed carefully to his feet. The ledge was nearly four feet wide at the point where he had reached it, but it narrowed as it climbed and for most of its length it seemed about a foot to eighteen inches in width. He began to move along it at once.

It was far easier going than he had dared to hope. The ledge was solid beneath his feet and his experience as a web-walker meant the narrow portions did not worry him at all. Even when he reached the first section where the ledge had crumbled, his luck was good, for portions of it remained, providing easy footholds to bridge the gap.

The second crumbled section was less easy. For about fifteen feet, the ledge had gone completely and Marcus was forced to climb upwards in a shallow arc to reach the other side. He was little more than halfway across when the rock spur he was holding gave way abruptly, throwing him outwards.

He actually dropped about three feet before his flailing left hand found a niche and gripped with all the strength of desperation. He swung like a short, slow pendulum, while the muscles of his left arm howled in protest.

Marcus glanced down. The ground seemed very, very far away. If he fell now, he might escape with broken bones, but he doubted it. He looked up. There was another handhold above him and to the right, well out of reach. He could see no toeholds at all.

His mind seemed to be working at lightning speed. He could not hold on for long. He could not throw himself on to the next section of the ledge – it was still too far away. There were no close holds.

Marcus found himself doing something that bordered on madness. He jerked his body to increase the pendulum swing. His grip faltered and a fingernail ripped in a sudden flair of agony. In that desperate instant he knew he had made a fearful mistake. His arm felt as if it was being dragged from its socket, his fingers were on fire. He could not hold on. He must fall.

His body arced. His right hand found the high hold. His foot caught a firm spur. His left hand came free, reached of its own accord and gripped a second spur. Marcus pressed his face against the cliff and wept with relief.

After several trembling minutes, he moved cautiously on, clambering sideways across the cliff-face like a crab. He felt the ledge with his feet, tested it, stood on it and offered a prayer of thanks to the Mother and Her Twins. He continued to shuffle sideways until the ledge widened and he was able to walk along almost normally. His entire body was trembling with fatigue and his backpack seemed to weigh a ton, but he had a feeling the worst was over.

The ledge climbed more steeply after that. It curved round two more promontories then stopped. Marcus looked up, hardly daring to breathe. To his right, the cliff-face climbed upwards, sheer for at least another fifty feet. But directly above him, within arm's reach, he could see the lip where this section of the cliff ended. He reached, gripped, swung himself upwards and moments later was seated, legs dangling, on a rocky plateau. He buried his face in his hands.

After a moment, Marcus climbed to his feet. He knew he had succeeded in the first leg of his mission. The plateau ran south for perhaps a quarter of a mile, then dipped and its stone surface gave way to undulating grassland. He was out of the crater in which Castle Dis now stood.

He turned back to the edge. Another cliff rose to his left now, but looking out from the one he had just climbed gave him a stunning view of the vast crater and its contents. Castle Dis now covered most of the ground surface, like a vast egg in a giant egg cup.

It was the first time he had seen the castle from above and it almost overwhelmed him. It stretched into the distance like a mighty city – a jumble of walls, towers, arches, streets, squares, aqueducts and roadways. For a long time he could find no meaning in the jumble, but his eyes gradually adjusted until he could clearly make out the Avenue of the Ateliers and the area near the Mutton Market with the entrance to his workstation.

From the Mutton Market, he swept his eye forward and quickly picked out the South Tower, which stood like a flat white finger pointing to the sky. Its slit windows were too narrow for him to see anyone within, but he knew they would be there, watching him from the turret room. The knowledge made him warm and nervous at the same time. It was a comfort to feel his friends were there, urging him on, but he felt the weight of responsibility upon him.

Marcus waved to his hidden friends and turned to go. As he did so, the spinner hit him from above.

Chapter Fifteen

She must have been clinging to the rising cliff-face on his right, for she dropped with such force that he was thrown violently on to the ground. The spinner was much larger than the one that attacked him in the silk pits. Her body alone was the size of a man and her long legs stood much higher. Marcus felt himself rolling towards the cliff edge and scrabbled at the rock to halt his momentum. Then the spinner hit him again.

Her movements were a blur of speed when she moved, but she moved in jerky bursts. Marcus had a fleeting impression of fangs and claws, then suddenly the spinner was still and he was staring into the black orbs of her eyes no more than eighteen inches from his own. He could see his face reflected in them, frozen in a mask of horror.

He kicked and caught the spinner on the underside of her bloated body. The creature twitched away from him, then hurled herself forward with such speed and ferocity that he had not even time to raise an arm. The foreclaw lashed towards him and he felt again the curiously painless numbing jolt as spinner poison pumped into his body. Like the last spinner, this one selected his shoulder for her attack. Like the last one, she attached a cable.

Marcus felt sick in his stomach. He knew that had he had the power of movement, he would have turned his head to vomit. As it was, he felt his limbs grow still. At the same time, his thoughts took on a familiar clarity as the venom coursed through his blood.

The spinner whirled and sprayed a mist of fluid from her tail-end that solidified into a net of filaments even as it touched him. She scuttled in a full circle around him, moving with almost preternatural speed. He felt the filaments wrapped around his body until he was enveloped in a sticky cocoon. He didn't understand what the spinner was doing, but a grisly suspicion was growing in his mind. He was being preserved alive to feed the spinner's hatchlings when they swarmed.

He became a giant egg, his arms pinned by his side, his legs locked together. Only his head remained free – a fortunate accident since he would certainly have suffocated had the spinner sprayed on to his face.

There was nothing he could do, no sound he could make. Blindly, he wondered if his friends could see what was happening. Not that it would make any difference if they could. He would be dead for sure long before they reached him, even if they were prepared to try.

The spinner ceased her spraying and, using four of her eight legs, began to roll him bodily towards the edge. Marcus watched the world revolve crazily, watched the edge approach closer and closer. There had to be something he could do, something he could try, something he could—

He tumbled over the edge and dropped like a stone.

Marcus jerked to a halt, then saw the cliff-face smash towards him. There was nothing he could do to save himself. He crashed into the cliff with enough force to break a dozen ribs, but the cocoon acted as a cushion so that he rebounded with scarcely worse than a bruise.

He swung, spun and ended suspended on his back from a single spinner cable. He watched the spinner herself crawl over the edge and start down the sheer cliff-face with a speed that was nothing short of astonishing. His own weight seemed not to make the slightest difference to her. He swung gently beneath her as she climbed and only moments later reached the crater floor as gently as if he had floated on thistledown.

The spinner dropped towards him, reeling in her cable as she came until she was standing astride him, a dark, looming shape from mankind's deepest nightmares. Using four of her legs she gripped him and drew him up towards her. In an instant that went beyond terror, he was pressed against her bloated underbelly. He could feel the warmth of the creature's body, her coarse body hair against his exposed cheek. His nostrils were filled with the dusky spinner smell.

She made slow passes with her legs, drawing more filaments from her body until he was literally tied to her. Then, without warning, she scuttled off across the rocks.

It was a bizarre, horrifying experience. Suspended beneath the spinner, Marcus could see the blur of her legs as she ran. There was a kaleidoscope of impressions from the front. Twisted plant groups fell away to each side, rocks rushed towards them on a collision course which changed to sudden sky as the spinner scuttled up and over them. He could not come to terms with the speed she travelled. He had worked with spinners for years, but only now did he learn how fast they could move.

It seemed only moments before he saw the gates of Castle Dis – an instant more before he was passing through them and speeding across the great empty courtyard immediately inside. Even in his panic, it occurred to him that when he left the castle, he had pushed the main gates shut, but when the spinner approached, they had both been thrown wide open. Who opened the gates for the spinner? He wondered if it would be the last question he would ever ask.

He thought she scuttled through to one of the main arterial roads, but quickly found he could no longer recognize the landmarks of Castle Dis, even in those areas with which he was most familiar. It was not just his insane position, suspended only inches from the ground beneath a spinner's belly. It was the fact that the spinner did not travel as he did, did not travel as a dog-cart or a horse or any human form of transport. She could move just as quickly sideways as forwards, and did so frequently. Sometimes she scurried around obstacles, sometimes she went straight over them.

For a long time she ran a beeline on a broad paved road, then switched to sideways motion to cross an open square. She turned into a narrow street and stopped abruptly. Between her front legs, Marcus could see a human figure standing in the street ahead, holding a naked sword. To his horror he recognized it as Prudence Rainwater.

Run! Marcus shrieked at her in his mind. *Run, Pru! The spinner will kill you!* But Pru did not run. Instead she advanced slowly towards the spinner, her sword raised.

Where had she found a sword? What was she trying to do? Where were the others? Question after question tumbled through his mind as panic grew to fever pitch.

'Let him go, you brute!' he heard Pru call. 'You let my Marcus go!'

The spinner moved. One moment it was stock still, watching. The next it was hurtling towards Pru at blinding speed. He actually caught the look of mute astonishment on her face as she tried to block the attack with her sword, then the spinner hit her, knocking her flying. He heard the sound of the sword clattering on the cobbles as the spinner hurried on.

Movement blurred as they raced through avenues, lanes and streets. They reached a square that looked familiar, then plunged into darkness. The spinner skittered sideways. He thought they must crash into a wall, but felt the world tilt suddenly. She was carrying him downwards. His mind began to race. Where was she taking him?

Suddenly he knew. They were on the catwalk of his workstation at the silk pits. The rushlights he lit had long since burned out, but one of the torches still spluttered feebly, casting a ghostly light. The spinner changed direction and he saw that the nets they had hung were ripped to shreds. He shivered. If they had remained in the station, they would all be dead.

For a moment he thought the spinner might head for the doorway into the station itself, but instead she climbed the rail of the catwalk and in a single, heart-stopping instant, plunged over the edge to drop into the pits themselves. All his senses, heightened by the spinner venom in his blood, told him they both must die. But then he noticed they were dropping slowly, not free falling, and decided the spinner must have attached a cable before she jumped. He watched the torchlight recede far above until eventually it blinked out altogether.

Marcus tilted again and realized the spinner had abandoned her cable to scamper down the sheer rock-face. He had passed beyond fear. All he hoped was that she would eat him quickly and he would not suffer too much pain.

He lost track of time. The spinner's motion never ceased, but in the total darkness he could only guess where they were going. He wondered how she could see. The Masters had always told him spinners had keen eyesight – the horseshoe arrangement of their eight eyes allowed them full-circle vision – but he had not known they could see in total darkness. The spinner ran downwards for so long he began to wonder about the old superstition that the silk pits were bottomless.

He saw light. Though dim, it gradually grew stronger until he could see the spinner's racing legs again and, eventually, make out something of his surroundings.

She ceased to climb downwards and scampered forward into a vast, high-roofed cavern. The light was low, steady as a glowglobe, but with a greenish tinge. He could not see its source.

The spinner stopped. She stood quite still. Despite his limited field of vision, Marcus could see stalagmite pillars rising from the floor, their surface encrusted with crystals that flashed and glittered.

The spinner stood on four of her eight legs and, to his horror, began to reach towards his body with the others. He felt a raking of her claws then was lowered slowly to the ground. He rolled on to his face and could see nothing but the rock on which he lay. He felt the spinner touch him again and again, but gently. Then he rolled over and over as the filaments which bound him were removed.

Marcus lay on his side, free of bindings, but still unable to move. From this angle he could see nothing but a corner of rock and two of the spinner's fragile legs. There was pain in his shoulder – the same shoulder she had cut to poison him. He wondered if her feast had started. Somehow he had imagined that being eaten alive would hurt a great deal more.

The spinner skittered back. He could see her now, crouched perhaps eight feet away from him, watching, her main eyes black with concentration. Something was happening to him. He could not be sure what, but his body felt . . . strange. He grew warm – so warm that he began to sweat. He reached up to wipe the sweat from his brow.

He could move!

Marcus tried to roll, tried to jump to his feet and run, but his body moved only sluggishly as if the poison was draining from his system slowly. It was not at all like this with Master Squat's leeches. He didn't know what was happening, except that *something* was.

He was aware that his head hurt. He felt a building pressure and a rhythmic, pounding pain which climbed to a peak, then gradually receded. As the pain disappeared, his mind cleared and his body came under control. He felt weak, his limbs trembled convulsively, but at least he could really move now. He turned, brought his legs slowly under him, then climbed on to his knees. He

143

waited for a moment, panting, reached for a pillar to support himself then scrambled painfully on to his feet. He stood teetering, but did not fall.

He was in a cavern that reminded him of Bishop Puddifat's cathedral. The high, arching roof seemed to generate its own light and closer to hand he recognized the source. On the rock-face to his left were patches of lichen which glowed green. It was a plant he had never seen before, something which must grow only in the depths of the silk pits.

There were few stalagmites, but those there were had formed a short, natural colonnade. Some joined up with stalactites descending from the roof to form slim, towering pillars. The crystal structures embedded in their surfaces made them look for all the world like glass. The eerie green light, the sparkling crystals, the pillared colonnade combined to make the cavern look man-made. He could imagine a procession led by Bishop Puddifat marching in stately fashion down that colonnade.

The spinner stood still as a statue three strides from him. She had watched him regain the use of his limbs, watched him climb painfully to his feet and was watching him now. What was she waiting for? He thought of a cat as it plays with a mouse, but he had never before seen a spinner toy with prey.

Dare he run? Marcus took an experimental step backwards and the spinner did not move. If he dare run, where would he run to? He was at the very bottom of the silk pits, on the floor of an abyss so deep it was almost unimaginable. It was insane to think he might somehow manage to climb out again, even if he could escape the spinner. Outside this cavern, there was not even light.

The spinner did not move. He could see her properly for the first time and chilled at her size. She was *far* larger than the brute that had poisoned him on the web. That spinner had been the size of a well-fed dog. This one stood nearly six feet off the floor on legs that were no thinner than his arm. She had the same bloated body, the same jointed head, the same eyes, fangs and claws as every spinner, but her colouring was almost beautiful. The entire body was covered in long, soft fur shimmering with multicoloured whorls, like oil on water.

She did not seem to breathe. Marcus took a second step backwards and felt his heel touch something hard. He glanced around to find himself close by a stubby limestone pillar. Beyond it ran a broad apron of rock which ended in a towering archway. Through the archway was darkness, which might have marked an exit from the cavern. In that instant, he would have swapped everything he had for a lighted torch.

He still had his sword! He glanced down to make sure, but he was right. The forgotten short sword was still sticking through his belt. Praying the spinner wouldn't move, he reached for it and drew it out. The spinner did not move.

Watching her carefully, Marcus began to edge away. The sword gave him confidence, although he knew that even with a weapon he would not last more than a moment if a spinner that size decided to attack. All the same, if he could escape her, he might just be able to hold his own against a smaller spinner.

Marcus edged along the rocky apron. Still the

spinner did not move. Was it possible he might escape? Her eyes flickered pearl grey for an instant, which meant her attention had wavered. She was no longer watching him as intently as before. He licked his lips and came to a decision. He turned to run towards the dark exit.

A second spinner scuttled from the archway. It stopped as Marcus froze. It was smaller than the one that brought him here, but not much. The body hair was pale grey, close to white, with a delicate stripe through it like a tabby cat.

There was the faintest sound of claw on rock. Marcus jerked round to find a third spinner had appeared to join the other too. It stood fifteen feet away, immobile now, but watching him.

A yellow-brown spinner emerged from the gloom beyond a pillar and stopped. Two more dropped down from the cavern roof, absorbed their cables back into their bodies, and stopped. He caught a movement from the corner of his eye, jerked round to find that fully seven spinners were now ranged to his right.

Slowly, Marcus turned. The spinner which scuttled from the archway had been joined by a dozen more. The outer reaches of the cavern were alive with sudden darting movements as spinner after spinner moved into the light. He counted a score . . . two score . . . then fifty, then lost count. He had never seen so many adult spinners at one time. Their sizes varied. Many were little larger than a mastiff, but at least one in three was as big as the spinner that had brought him. They sported different colourings and markings. Each scuttled into the light and stopped.

Marcus felt his sword handle slick with sweat. He was surrounded. There were more spinners in this single cavern than the Masters believed existed in the entire silk pits. Those at the front skittered forward a few steps in response to pressure from behind as their numbers continued to increase. Marcus stood solitary in the centre of the rocky apron with the spinners ringed around him. Wherever he turned, he looked out across a sea of spinners.

There was no more movement on the outskirts of the horde. Everywhere he looked there were immobile spinners. Everywhere he looked their eyes were black, which meant they were watching him. Watching him for what? Were they waiting for him to make a move?

There was a stillness in the cavern that chilled his blood. Had he the courage to plunge in and fight? It would be death, but at least a swift death. Marcus hefted the sword. He took a deep breath.

And then he heard the singing.

Chapter Sixteen

It swept over him, sweet, pure, clear and familiar. The soprano cadences swooped and soared to touch his heart despite the nightmare death so close. Marcus stood open-mouthed and listened. This time the singing did not fade.

He could hear it in his ears. He could hear it in his head. It was as if the singing rose inside his skull and flowed out into the gloomy cavern. It was the same song he heard so often in the mornings, but richer, more meaningful, more beautiful. It gave him joy.

Some instinct told him the spinners could hear it too. They stood, unmoving, watching him intently with their round black eyes.

The singing curled around him, stroking him, caressing him, soothing him like a mother's lullaby. Despite his earlier intent, he lowered the sword. He felt his body relax, his fear ease. The singing was so wonderful he almost smiled.

It was the spinners who were singing!

The realization struck him like a body blow. The creatures were singing in his *mind*! He thought he heard the singing outside himself, but it was really inside. The singing was a waking dream.

He looked at the surrounding spinners. They were the most dangerous creatures on the face of Pradesh, the most ugly, terrifying horrors to crawl beneath the earth, yet their singing was beautiful. The song was calling him, luring him. He wanted to dance and shout and run towards the singing. He wanted to embrace the spinners.

A worm of doubt crawled into his stomach. Was this a way in which the spinners enticed their prey? Down here in the depths, did they forgo their webs? The thought chilled him. He could feel a different sensation in his body, like the poison paralysis, but softer. He could still move, but he no longer wanted to. It was as if, somehow, he was being . . . prepared. But for what?

There was something coming. He could feel it in his mind, a force so powerful it almost swamped his fear. The singing rose to a crescendo. There was movement, rustling, clicking, as the sea of spinners parted before the most astonishing creature he had ever seen.

She was a spinner herself, but so gigantic that she dwarfed every other spinner in the cavern. She was easily twice the size of the largest among them and the largest among them was bigger than a dray-horse. Her head alone was broader than Marcus's shoulders. Her legs were thicker than his body. She was covered in a fine grey fur. He found himself thinking of Helgageerd, the great spinner who had terrorized the realm of King Wolfgruff.

The monster stopped no more than fifteen feet away. Her eyes turned black as they focused on him. He was vaguely aware that the remaining spinners kept a respectful distance from the giant. The singing tailed into a single elongated chord, then stopped. Marcus stared up open-mouthed at the spinner queen.

A huge clawed leg raised, then reached out for him. Without an instant's hesitation, Marcus hacked at it with his sword.

The blade bit and the leg jerked back, oozing a

dark fluid that seemed too black for blood. Marcus flung himself forward and cut again, this time at the body of the giant insect. The sword struck, though to what effect he could not tell for his foot caught a loose stone and he tumbled heavily. His head struck the rock apron in a blinding flash of pain and for a moment all went black.

He came to almost at once in a mêlée of movement. The spinners were pressed around their wounded queen in a heaving carpet so dense that she had almost disappeared. Marcus turned his head, groaning, and began slowly to scramble to his feet. Then he saw her again, lifted by the remaining spinners, carried bodily, huge though she was, towards the gloomy recesses at the back of the cavern.

Marcus was on his feet now, swaying. But no spinner attacked him, no spinner came close. He shook his head violently to clear it and was rewarded by a jab of pain. Yet pain or not, he felt steadier. His hand, clutched convulsively around the hilt of his sword, was slick with sweat. He looked around. The nearest spinner was more than thirty feet away. He ran, uttering a prayer to the Mother and Her Twins that they might aid him in escaping the nightmare.

He dived into an opening in the rock wall and found himself in a narrow fissure, dark but with the greenish glow of lichen at the end. He ran to the light, squeezed out into a cave so heavily coated with the lichen that he could see almost as well as he would in daylight. Marcus stopped. In the centre of the cavern was a statue of a spinner.

He stared. The statue was cast in bronze and looked ancient beyond belief. It was crudely worked, standing almost six feet high. All eight eyes were missing, but otherwise it seemed in good repair. He looked around. There were other signs that this cavern had been shaped by men. The floor was cut in broad, square flagstones and there were archaic hieroglyphs cut into the walls.

Almost at once he saw the doorway. It was set into the right-hand wall, a solid affair of oak studded with iron and secured by an old-fashioned mechanical latch. Heart pounding, Marcus crept forward, hesitated, then opened the door.

He was at the bottom of a float-shaft. Although he had only ever seen one before, he recognized it instantly. The magical symbols were cut deep into the walls, the tube soared high above him like a chimney, its surface so smooth it seemed almost liquid. Open-mouthed, Marcus stepped inside.

In normal times he would only have to place his palm on the appropriate symbol for the magic of the float-shaft to carry him smoothly upwards. But since magic no longer worked, all he had was a shaft. But a shaft that went where? It could only lead out of the pits. Nothing else made sense.

Marcus began to shake. Here was escape, if he could only find a way to use it. He stared upwards. Was it possible to climb? There were no handholds, but the shaft was narrow: float-shafts were seldom designed to carry more than two people standing side by side. If he could prop his back against one side and his feet flat against the other, he might be able to work his way upwards.

To his surprise, it was easy. The smooth surface of the shaft actually helped, for while his feet seemed to grip firmly, his back pushed upwards almost without friction.

The floor of the shaft had disappeared into darkness before he realized his mistake. He was now high up and tiring rapidly. His legs had begun to ache and trembled alarmingly each time he tried to move them. He had no idea how much further he had to go, except that his memory of the nightmare journey underneath the spinner suggested it must be a long way.

After ten minutes more, Marcus knew his mistake was fatal. He was now so tired he could not move another inch; so tired that it was only a matter of time before his leg muscles gave out and he plunged downwards to his death. He closed his eyes and began to pray. Halfway through the prayer, he discovered he had lost all sensation below the waist. His body took on a will of its own and he felt it relax. His feet lost contact with the wall of the shaft and he fell—

Floated!

Marcus did not fall. He was hanging in the middle of the shaft, as perfectly suspended as if magic had never ceased to work. But if he was suspended, magic must still be working, at least inside this shaft. There was no way he could float otherwise. He shook his head to clear it of the puzzle. Whether magic worked or not was the last thing he needed to think upon just now. He was alive, which meant there was a chance he might still escape the spinner pits. He scrabbled at the smooth walls to pull himself upwards.

It was painfully slow going, but at least he could stop and rest, floating gently as a feather in the narrow shaft. On his third rest period he noticed that he actually continued to drift upwards now, but painfully slowly. He rested, then dragged himself upwards, rested, then dragged himself upwards . . .

There was light above. Not the leprous green of the silk pits' lichen, but clean white light, like daylight. It gave him a burst of energy so that he clambered like a mad thing, face almost pressed against the smooth wall. He reached the light, saw the walls of the shaft turn transparent as he emerged from the pit. He was in a room, inside the glassy tube the shaft had become. He turned, panting, to look around.

He was not alone.

Marcus flung himself backwards with a stifled scream. Beside him in the shaft, so close it could reach out and touch him, was the demon he had seen in the Wizards' Guildhall. The creature was exactly as he remembered: the same floor-length cloak, the same black insectile body, the same plump, flabby face, the same tiny pointed teeth and rosebud mouth. It turned towards him.

Marcus felt a terror rise in him far beyond anything the spinners had induced. He felt weak and ill, his stomach convulsing uncontrollably. Only the fact that he had not eaten for hours stopped him being sick. There was nowhere he could escape. The thing had only to reach out to touch him, only to . . .

The demon turned away and began to claw at the inside of the transparent tube, exactly as it had done when Marcus watched it from the outside. Then the tube itself grew cloudy, milky and opaque. As it did so, to Marcus's profound astonishment, the creature faded, dimmed, then vanished.

For a long moment he stood, scarcely able to believe his luck, still weak with fear, not understanding what had happened. Then his paralysis broke and he looked around in panic for a way to leave the tube.

The milkiness began to clear. As it did so, the demon form returned, grimacing and clawing at the inside of the tube. It turned towards him, the same malignant expression on its features, lips parted to show the pearl needles of teeth. As fear flowered in him, the creature looked away, clawed at the tube again, then faded exactly as it had done before.

Exactly as it had done before.

Marcus took a deep breath to calm his pounding heart. He waited. Sure enough, the demon reappeared to repeat the same movements again before disappearing. No demon this, but an illusion! A phantasm set to frighten those who might intrude into the shaft. It had to be maintained by magic and magic no longer worked . . . except that magic *did* work, some magic at least, otherwise he could not be floating in the shaft.

The demon reappeared, clawed, turned, clawed, disappeared.

An illusion for certain – one which barred the way. Which meant there was a way to be barred – a way in – and out – for those with the knowledge and courage to take it. Nothing else made sense. The demon reappeared, clawed, turned, clawed, disappeared.

All it needed was courage. Marcus waited, heart pounding despite a series of deep breaths. The demon – not a demon, just an *illusion* – reappeared. Marcus pushed against the tube behind him and floated towards the thing. Was it an illusion? He had an instant of doubt – the demon seemed so real – then he reached it, passed through it and found himself, shaking with relief, in the room outside the pillar.

'Well,' said a voice behind him, 'that was an impressive trick!'

Chapter Seventeen

Erasmus Squat was lounging on a sofa, a tall glass of amber sembala in one hand and an open bottle on the floor beside him. He seemed to have risen in the world since the day he leeched the spinner poison out of Marcus. He was wearing a long brocade jacket, richly ornamented in gold and silver thread. A floppy-brimmed black hat and a silver-topped wolf's-head cane had been thrown carelessly on to a nearby chair. He waved a languid hand towards the bottle. 'Care for a drink? The wizards keep a fine distillate.'

Marcus blinked. 'Thank thee, no, Dr Squat. I be too young for sembala.'

Squat's eyes narrowed. 'Have we met, or has my fame made me recognizable?'

'Don't you remember, sir? You cured me of the spinner poison.'

Squat stared at him blearily for a long moment. 'The 'prentice from the silk pits!' he exclaimed at length. 'What's your name, boy? My memory isn't what it used to be.'

'Mustard,' Marcus said. 'Marcus Mustard.'

'Well, Master Mustard, we find ourselves in something of a pickle, do we not?' Squat asked. 'May I assume you know what's happened to our mighty Castle Dis?'

'The 'Freshing moved the castle and left the people,' Marcus said, echoing Pru's theory. He wondered how Squat had stayed with the castle. Perhaps he'd been underground as well.

Squat looked up at him in surprise. 'So you worked it out – clever lad!' He took a long drink from his glass. 'Now tell me how to get them back together again.'

'I don't know,' Marcus said glumly.

'In that case, dear boy, enlighten me as to how you happened to be lurking in that pillar and how you survived the demon.'

'Bain't no demon,' Marcus said. 'It be an illusion, so I just walked through it.'

Squat took this information without comment. He drained his glass then stared into it as if searching for flies in the bottom.

'Sir,' Marcus said, 'we be in the Pooka Ginid.'

If the information phased Squat, he did not show it. He lifted his empty glass in mock toast. 'Then here's to the Pooka Ginid, Master Mustard!' Marcus wondered if he knew what the place was.

'I was trying to get help,' Marcus said. 'But a spinner got me.'

To his astonishment, Squat giggled. 'What a talent you have for irritating spinners! But at least you don't look as sickly as you did when we last met.'

'She didn't bite me,' Marcus told him sourly. He was certain Dr Squat was drunk and could feel anger rising. He took a deep breath and tried to make his voice sound urgent. 'Dr Squat,' he said, 'we be in the Pooka Ginid. There be spinners in the castle and the hatchling swarm is due. We got to get help, you and I!'

'You, perhaps, but not I,' Squat said. 'I prefer it here. No guardians of the Law to harass me, no fear of jail, no rules and regulations, good distillate and fine clothes for the taking.' He smiled benignly. 'Now I even have the company of Master Mustard, apprentice extraordinary. At least, until he rushes off to find help or become a spinner's breakfast.'

'It bain't safe!' Marcus was almost shouting in his frustration. 'Big spinners might not get in here, but hatchlings will. Once swarm starts we could be ate in minutes!'

'Not in here,' Squat said flatly. 'You're in the headquarters of the Wizards' Guild, my boy. Enough fine food and drink to keep us going for a lifetime. And magical protections that would turn a tyrannosaur.'

Marcus was beginning to wonder why he was wasting his time – except that Squat had saved his life. 'Magic don't work no more,' he said patiently. 'Not even in here. I was here, down in the cells, and that's how I got out after the 'Freshing. Cell locks stopped working.' *But the float shaft still works*, a small voice whispered in his mind.

'Indeed they did,' Squat agreed, 'for was I not in those same cells – possibly no more than a few doors down from you, dear boy, and certainly a great deal the worse for distillate. But whatever the state of play elsewhere – and I grant you that elsewhere the workability of magic leaves much to be desired – magic continues to work perfectly well here.' He gestured towards the transparent pillar where the insectile monster clawed to get out. 'Did you not tell me that demon creature is an illusion? A *magical* illusion?'

It was true. At least two spells had functioned in the shaft – the float spell that had kept Marcus from falling and the spell that maintained the demon illusion. 'Yes, but—' Marcus began uncertainly.

Squat waved a languid hand and the bottle levitated from the floor, floated towards him, then tilted to fill up his glass. 'Is that not a perfectly functional spell?' he asked as the bottle floated back.

'I don't understand,' Marcus said.

'Then permit me to enlighten you,' Squat said; and for the first time, a sour note crept into his voice. 'What you witness, dear boy, is a fine example of crumbling values. Once this great fortress of ours was dedicated to decency, tradition and moral fibre. A long time ago, admittedly, but that's progress for you. Now, I fear, it is dedicated only to the pursuit of power. At least, by Lord Ruslan.'

'Lord Ruslan?' Marcus echoed. He shivered. He remembered the chill glare of Lord Alan Ruslan all too well.

'A man far above us in station, Master Mustard, but one with ambitions to climb higher still. The Wizard Earl seeks to overthrow the Alizarin Emperor himself.'

Marcus stared at him.

'Outside of this Guildhall and one or two other places, magic no longer works,' said Squat easily. 'What happens when magic ceases to work? The entire fabric of our society begins to fall apart. There is panic in the streets – or there would be if there were anybody left in the streets. Who gets the blame? Our beloved leader, Leon Dark – that's what leaders are for in times of trouble. So the mob turns on Lord Dark, hangs him, jails him, casts him into exile – the details hardly matter so long as he is removed from office. At which point Alan

Ruslan reveals he knows a way to get the magic working again and a grateful populace offers him the throne. Which he accepts with enormous reluctance, but accepts nonetheless and *poof!* we have a new Alizarin Emperor.' He drank deeply from the glass.

'But how would Lord Ruslan get magic to work again?'

'By breaking the crystals he made to interfere with it.'

For a long moment Marcus said nothing. He licked his lips. 'Lord Ruslan stopped the magic working?' He was remembering how he had trusted his spellbell, how he had climbed on to the spinner's web.

'I shall not bore you with the details,' Squat told him, 'largely because I do not have them. But it has long been known that certain crystals modify the action of magic. The Wizard Earl managed to grow some that switch it off altogether. They have been hidden at strategic points in Castle Dis.'

'How do you know this?' Marcus gasped. It seemed as likely as Prunebane's claim to be the son of Bishop Puddifat.

Squat shrugged. 'He kept a diary. I found it in the pocket when I stole his coat.'

Chapter Eighteen

What to do? What to do? It was now two hours since Marcus had emerged from the float shaft, two hours nearer the beginning of the hatchling swarm. He was still in the Wizards' Guildhall without the slightest idea what to do. He stared at the prostrate figure of Squat in panic and disgust. The doctor had finished the last of his bottle half an hour ago and had been snoring since, his mouth hung open to reveal a broken tooth. There would be little help from that quarter.

Squat grunted and rolled over, then suddenly opened both eyes. He stared at Marcus as if he had never seen him before. 'Who are you?'

'Marcus,' Marcus said. 'Marcus Mustard.'

Squat started to push himself upright. 'Oh, yes – the spinners' friend. You came up from the shaft. Where does it lead, incidentally?' He seemed a lot more in control of himself than he had been.

Marcus said, 'Into the pits. Below them, really.'

Squat took his head in his hands and squeezed it firmly. Then he looked at Marcus. 'More underhand work by our respected wizards, I'll warrant. Did we talk much, Master Mustard?'

'Talk?'

'While I was inebriated. I fear my recollection is . . . incomplete.'

'Yes, sir, we talked a little.'

'Did I tell you of Lord Ruslan's scheme?'

'Yes, sir.'

Squat fished a silver pill-box from a pocket of his brocade jacket, flipped open the lid and popped two crimson pellets into his mouth. He waited for a moment, then blinked and shook himself violently. 'By the Mother!' he exclaimed. He closed the pill-box and put it away. 'An invention of my own,' he explained. 'Foul stuff, but wonderful for unscrambling brains.' He sniffed, as if to clear his head. 'Now, Master Mustard, we must decide what to do.'

'Sir?' frowned Marcus. The last time the question had arisen, Squat had said bluntly that he proposed to do nothing.

'As I understand it, Marcus – I may call you Marcus, may I not, having once saved your life? – as I understand it, Marcus, you and I are the only people on the face of Pradesh who know of Ruslan's foul activities. With such knowledge comes responsibility, does it not? Do you know why this is so?'

Sober, Dr Squat made Marcus more nervous even than he had while drunk. 'For the common good?' he ventured uneasily.

'Don't be silly, boy – for our own advantage! Have you any idea of the stakes at issue here? The throne of Dis, position, power and wealth beyond the dreams of avarice! If we can't cut ourselves a slice of that little pie, we must have the brains of newts. As I see it, we have four options. One, we let Ruslan know we have evidence of his filthy scheme and demand vast quantities of gold to keep quiet about it. Then two—'

'But that's blackmail!' Marcus protested, appalled.

'I see you're familiar with the activity,' Squat said dryly. 'Two, we report Ruslan's scheme to Leon Dark and trust in his generosity for a fat reward. Naive, I know, but we must at least *consider* all options. Three, we search out the crystals, hide them somewhere else, then present ourselves as the saviours of humanity. In effect, we take over Ruslan's scheme and run it for ourselves. Was that three? Then four—'

'We can't do that!' Marcus protested. 'It's—' He had been about to say, *It's not right* when it occurred to him that Squat would not care. Instead he said, 'We don't know enough about magic to make it work.'

'A weakness, I grant you. Which leaves us with four: we offer to bring magic back, then destroy the crystals. The gratitude of the great unwashed will guarantee us rich rewards. I shall be permitted to practise medicine again. They may even make me a knight. You will probably get enough money to buy your own spinners.'

The man was clearly insane. 'Dr Squat,' Marcus said urgently, 'we be in the Pooka Ginid. The whole castle be in the Pooka Ginid. The caves are stuffed with spinner eggs and the hatchling swarm is due. There be nobody else in the whole castle as I knows of save me and thee and my friends. We have no horse, we have no—'

'Friends?' Squat put in. 'Did you say friends?'

'Barricaded in the South Tower. I think they will be safe from the hatchlings. We have no—'

'How many friends?' Squat asked urgently.

Marcus blinked. 'There be Prunebane and Cloydd, Pru Rainwater and Molestrangler.' He counted in his head and announced, 'Four.'

'With yourself five and myself six!' exclaimed

Squat excitedly. He reached out to take hold of Marcus's shoulders and shook him. 'By the Holy Mother, Master Mustard, this means we can hold our own Refreshing!'

Chapter Nineteen

'I don't like this, Dr Squat,' Marcus muttered sourly. It was the understatement of his life. They were walking across the South Plaza to the tower that housed his friends. So far they had not met a spinner and so far the hatchling swarm had not begun. Squat did not seem worried by either possibility, but Marcus was terrified. He had his sword ready in his hand and his eyes darted towards every shadow. Squat, by contrast, strode ahead as if he had not a care in the world. Lord Ruslan's stolen coat billowed out behind him.

'You worry too much, Master Mustard,' Squat called over his shoulder. 'Have you no sense of destiny?'

Something moved in a doorway and Marcus leapt into a defensive posture, but it was a rat, not a spinner. He lowered his sword sheepishly.

'I must compound you some nerve nostrum,' Squat remarked, grinning.

They passed the obsidian statue of Lord Dark and Marcus noticed the marvellous sheets of colour no longer played around it. It seemed that Prunebane's new-fangled 'lectricity was something that did not last long.

They reached the quartz-faced tower. The doors were shut. 'They may be barred,' Marcus said. He himself had instructed his friends to bar the doors. He pushed them experimentally. They were barred.

Squat, who had been staring up at the statue

of Lord Dark, said, 'Knock, boy, knock! You said yourself it's dangerous to hang around outside.'

Marcus knocked without protest, but he was worried his friends might not hear him. They would not be expecting his return. Pru had seen him carried away by the spinner. They would be certain he was dead by now. He knocked again.

'What's the matter?' Squat asked irritably. The sight of the obsidian Lord Dark seemed to have put him in ill humour.

'The room we sealed be high up,' Marcus told him. He thumped the door again in a desultory manner, wondering how on earth they were going to attract his friends' attention. To his surprise, he heard the sound of a bolt drawn, then the door was flung open.

'Marcus!' screamed Pru Rainwater. 'You be alive! You be alive!' She flung herself upon him and, to his profound embarrassment, covered his face with kisses.

Marcus extricated himself with difficulty. 'This be my friend, Prudence Rainwater,' he muttered to Squat, blushing furiously.

'Mistress Rainwater!' Squat exclaimed. He seized her hand and bowed, as if in the presence of a queen. 'Erasmus Squat at your service, my dear.' He kissed her fingers, then released the hand.

'Why, sir—' Pru simpered, obviously delighted. She dropped a curtsey. 'It be nice to meet with you, good sir.'

'Dr Squat saved me from the spinner poison,' Marcus said by way of explanation. 'He wants us—' He stopped, deciding he would wait before mentioning what Dr Squat wanted them to do.

Prudence, in any case, was less than interested. She fussed them through the door in a barrage of questions about his escape from the spinner and ushered them upstairs to the room where the others were waiting. 'Hatchling swarm bain't started yet,' remarked little Cloydd excitedly. He appeared not at all surprised to find Marcus still alive.

The others were far more curious and it was nearly an hour before they would allow him to explain what Squat wanted them to do. Throughout it all, Squat sat patiently in high good humour as Pru served him soup and pressed him to delicacies of soft cheese, cubed and sprinkled in a variety of spices. But it came at length to the point of telling. 'The Doctor wants us to take part in a Refreshing.'

They stared at him, thunderstruck. For a long moment there was total silence, then they all began to talk at once.

'We bain't p-p-priests nor wa-wa-wa-wizards!'

''Freshing's what got us in this mess!'

''Freshing didn't w-w-work right last time.'

'Magic don't work now, Marcus.'

'Spinners be out there now the spells is—'

'—swarm soon—'

'—can't do it, Marcus, not us. We—'

It was Squat who calmed them. 'My *dear* friends,' he said with such emphasis that they all fell silent. 'There are difficulties to be sure, but none are insurmountable.' He smiled and rubbed his hands together, interlocking the fingers then cracking each, one after another. Marcus noticed for the first time how long they were. 'Let me deal with some of your objections. First, Master Molestrangler, it is perfectly correct to suggest the Refreshing did not work as planned last time. But that was because it was held in the open where

167

Lord Ruslan's crystals could interfere with the magic. We shall not repeat that mistake.'

''Freshing's got to be held in the open,' Peter Prunebane put in. ''Freshing's *always* held in the open.'

'Not so,' said Squat easily. 'It has generally been held in the open so that more people might attend. But I can recall two occasions – before any of you were born, I fear – when it was held, quite successfully, inside. As to your other objections, we do indeed need at least one wizard, but I myself have had some magical experience – part of my medical training, you appreciate. Priests are not necessary, whatever they may claim to the contrary. In this, as in most things, they remain a parasitic profession.'

'Magic don't work now, Dr Squat,' Pru Rainwater said again, gently enough, but insistently.

Squat turned a brilliant smile on her. 'I appreciate your reminding me, lovely lady. But there remain parts of Castle Dis where magic continues to function. The Wizards' Guildhall is one of them and it is there that I plan to hold the ceremony.'

Marcus frowned. There had been something at the back of his mind for quite a while now and it surfaced suddenly. 'Can we trust magic to work at the Guildhall?' he asked. 'Didn't work in the cells underneath.' He looked at Squat. 'Else you and I would not be free.'

'That thought concerned me for some time, Marcus,' Squat said seriously. 'Then I recalled that the cells are *not* below the Guildhall – not directly below, that is. One approaches them along a corridor which runs some distance south of the hall itself. Evidently they lie within the influence of Ruslan's crystals, but as you and

I have witnessed, Marcus, the hall itself does not.'

Cloydd, who had said nothing throughout the entire discussion, suddenly put in, 'When shall we do it, sir? I wants to go home.'

Marcus knew what Cloydd meant. They were still in the castle, still in the place they had called home all their lives, but it didn't feel like home. It felt strange and threatening. Cloydd wanted it back the way it was.

'I propose we should attempt the Refreshing as soon as possible,' Squat said. 'My studies suggest it is possible with six participants and fortunately there are six of us, so there is no reason why we should not succeed. I—'

'B-b-but wa-wa-we ah-don't know wa-wa-what to ah-do!' exclaimed Molestrangler, nervousness causing his stammer to flood.

'I shall instruct you,' Squat said easily. He turned away as if dismissing Molestrangler's objection and said to Peter Prunebane, 'Now you, Master Prunebane, you raised the question of the spinners and that indeed is a problem. We must get safely to the Wizards' Guildhall, which fortunately is not too far away, and since Marcus and I arrived here in one piece, one might suppose it not too dangerous a trip. But that assumes we get there before the hatchling swarm begins and none of us can predict when that will be, so I suggest we start out straightaway.' He looked around. 'Who's with me?'

'I am,' Cloydd said promptly. He smiled eagerly at his friends.

Chapter Twenty

'Dr Squat . . . ?' Marcus murmured thoughtfully as they walked the empty streets of Castle Dis. They had formed a line by twos, the better to watch out for spinners. Except for Prudence Rainwater, each was now armed with a poisoned dagger, courtesy of the doctor who 'happened to have them about his person'. Pru, who had refused to have anything to do with poison, carried a spiked mace she found in the guardroom of the tower. The expression on her face suggested she would not hesitate to use it.

'Yes, Marcus?' Squat responded easily.

'Are you sure the protection spells on the Wizards' Guildhall will keep out hatchlings?'

'I see no reason why they should not,' Squat shrugged. 'Wizards are no fonder of spinners than the rest of us. You may be certain their protections are of the highest quality.'

Marcus frowned. 'Not *spinners*, Dr Squat. Not full-grown spinners – *hatchlings*. See, the castle never landed in the Pooka Ginid before, so there weren't no need to guard against a hatchling swarm.'

Squat looked thoughtful. 'You may have something there, Marcus. You may indeed.'

The conversation must have been on his mind when they reached the Wizards' Guildhall, for he took care to secure the door behind them and checked all outer doors and windows. Then he led the group into a small anteroom which Marcus had not seen before. Plain white linen robes hung from hooks along one wall like a row of empty wizards.

'My friends,' Squat said cheerfully, 'it seems important to begin as soon as possible, so I suggest we begin right away. Please find yourself a robe that fits and put it on.'

'I bain't undressing in front of men!' Pru Rainwater exclaimed promptly. She glared at Dr Squat.

'Calm yourself, Mistress Rainwater – there is no need for anyone to undress. The robes are drawn on over our normal garb. So make sure to pick one large enough.'

Marcus felt peculiar in his robe. Simple though it was, it was still the richest garment he had ever worn. Worse still, it oozed magic, making his skin crawl. He felt self-conscious, silly and more than a little frightened, but when he looked at the others they had actually taken on an air of dignity. If he had not known their faces, he might have believed he had stumbled into a wizards' convention.

'Come,' Squat said when everyone was ready. 'Follow me!' He led them through a doorway into the most astonishing chamber Marcus had ever seen.

Marcus stared around in wonderment. Huge high windows looked out on to the empty street, but a peculiar patterning of the glass told him they would appear a plain stone wall to anyone looking in. Which was perhaps as well, for the chamber was so richly ornamented it would have drawn thieves like a magnet. Cloth of gold curtained the walls and adorned the ceiling. The floor was a chequerboard mosaic of obsidian and silver tiles. To the east were two bulbous pillars ornamented in gold and silver, inlaid with a series of mythic scenes. The whole place reeked of magic, but nowhere more strongly than the pillars where the inlays writhed and crawled to bring the myths alive.

Between the pillars suspended on fine silver chains was an enormous circular mirror of polished amethyst, set in an electrum frame. Shapes swam and twisted in its depths.

Directly in front of the pillars was a black-draped altar in the shape of a double cube. Neatly laid out on it was a gem-encrusted chalice, a slim silver blade and a short bamboo wand, ornamented at one end with a carving painted to represent flame. Beside the wand was a brass disc, inscribed in mystic symbols. Beyond it, in a brazen bird-cage, was a tiny winged demon which glared at them malevolently.

'Don't touch anything,' warned Dr Squat. 'This sort of place can get you into trouble.' He walked to the altar, lifted the edge of the cloth and produced six parchment scrolls from a shallow cupboard underneath. 'This is the Refreshing ritual,' he said soberly as he handed one to each member of the group. 'All you have to do is follow what it says and speak aloud any words underlined in red.' He smiled reassuringly. 'Before you know it, we shall all be back at Jubal Distala to a heroes' welcome.'

Prudence stared at her scroll as if it were a poisonous snake. After a moment she said, 'I bain't never learned to read High Pradesh.'

'M-m-me neither,' Molestrangler muttered. High Pradesh was the liturgical script reserved for ceremonial.

Squat blinked, then frowned. 'Can any of you read it?'

The others turned to look at Marcus. He bit his bottom lip. 'I can, Doctor, excepting for long words and such. Cloydd can't read at all.'

'I read it a little,' Prunebane said. 'My father taught me – Bishop Puddifat.'

'Only a little,' Marcus emphasized, ignoring the familiar claim of parentage. 'I be the only one here can read it proper.' A thought struck him. "Cept maybe you, Dr Squat.'

Squat cast his eyes briefly heavenwards. 'In that case, Marcus, you and I must lead the rest, prompting them when necessary and instructing them on what to do. I'm sure it will work just as well.' He sounded confident, but Marcus noticed his fingers were twisted in the Sign of the Horns for good luck.

Marcus glanced at his scroll. *Congregation to the East*, it began. Did that mean those taking part – Dr Squat, Prunebane, Molestrangler, Cloydd, Pru and himself – or those who, in a normal 'Freshing, came to watch? *High Priest's homily (optional)*. But they had no High Priest. Unless Dr Squat planned to take that rôle. *Archond intones*. What was an Archond? What did he – it? – intone. *Scrunflangler responds*. Scrunflangler? What in the name of the Mother and Her Holy Twins was a Scrunflangler?

Then, blood chilling, Marcus found a phrase underlined in red, which meant he had to speak it aloud. The phrase was *Sqagg xlft loft possum sghbkkl nagghct*. 'Dr Squat—' said Marcus quickly. 'Dr Squat—?'

But Dr Squat had already stepped towards the altar to begin the ritual.

For Marcus, the next hour was a nightmare. Squat elevated the chalice and began the invocation of the Twins. He seemed to have a talent for

173

the Art. Serpents of amber light began to crawl and flicker in the amethyst mirror between the pillars.

'I don't like this,' Pru Rainwater muttered sourly. She was still clutching her kitchen club.

'Shh!' Marcus hushed her urgently. He knew little of magic, but what he did know convinced him it was dangerous to interrupt a ceremony, especially if you were taking part in it.

'Can you read this scroll?' asked Prunebane in a whisper. 'I can't make sense of it. Bain't me, Marcus – it's the scroll. It be in a foreign tongue.'

'He said he would tell you what to say!' hissed Marcus. 'And when.'

'If he don't, will you, Marcus?' Prunebane asked plaintively.

'Yes! Yes, I will. Now will you be quiet!'

'Sorry, Marcus.'

'Place now the dagger of my Art within my grasp,' commanded Dr Squat. He held out one hand in readiness.

Molestrangler, whose part was to hand him the dagger, ran forward in panic and bumped the altar with such violence that the brazen disc clattered across the floor. Molestrangler made to dive after it, but Squat stopped him with an angry glare. 'Leave it, boy, leave it! Hand me the damned dagger!'

Molestrangler returned to the altar and sheepishly handed him the dagger. 'S-s-s-sorry.'

'Do you reckon he knows what he be doing?' asked Pru Rainwater suspiciously.

'Who – Raymond?'

'Nay, not Raymond – I knows Raymond don't know what he be doing – I mean the doctor!'

Marcus, who was afraid to *shh* her as he would his male friends, said in a voice so low it barely carried beyond his nose, 'Course he knows what he be doing!'

'What?' Pru asked loudly.

'He knows! He knows!' Marcus told her desperately.

'Only if he don't know what he be doing, it could be bad for all of us,' Pru said, unwilling to leave it alone. 'Look what happened at the last 'Freshing and that was done by proper made-up wizards. Priests too.'

Marcus decided to ignore her.

'Who stands in place of Serpigal, the first-born Twin?' intoned Dr Squat.

'No need to sulk,' Pru Rainwater said to Marcus. 'I'm sure we're all doing us best.'

'Who stands in place of Serpigal, the first-born Twin?'

Marcus realized suddenly it was the second time Dr Squat had asked the ritual question. 'That be you, Jacob!' he hissed at Cloydd.

A stricken look crossed the albino's face and he began to weep. Squat cast his eyes to heaven. 'What's the matter, boy?'

'I don't know what I be supposed to say!' Cloydd howled.

Marcus glanced at his scroll. '"I stand in place of Serpigal,"' he prompted.

'Then it's you to speak, Marcus,' Cloydd wailed.

It got no better as the ritual went on. Yet despite missed cues, dropped implements and one ghastly moment when Molestrangler almost managed to demolish a pillar, Marcus watched the familiar lightning play of magic overhead. Perhaps Dr Squat was a far better wizard than

175

he pretended. Whatever the reason, against all odds, the spell seemed to be working.

'My f-f-foot!' moaned Molestrangler as he dropped a ritual sword, fortunately hilt first, on his shoe.

'I, Erasmus Squat, command the Elements to transport our fortress to the hallowed site of Jubal Distala!' screamed Squat loudly enough to drown out any other sound.

There was a moment of deep silence. A soft plop on the nearest window caused Marcus to turn his head. A tiny spinner, no larger than a groat coin, was clinging to the glass. He stared at it blankly: he had never seen a spinner so small. Then he knew. This was not an adult spinner but a hatchling. It was the first dark drop of rain before a storm. The swarm had begun.

Marcus closed his eyes and prayed. In a moment the tiny spinner would be joined by another, then a dozen others, then a score, then thousands. They would pass like a tidal wave across every building in the castle and for all Squat's talk of magical protections, Marcus doubted there was anything that could really keep them out of the Guildhall. Unless the Refreshing worked, unless the castle moved at once, they were doomed.

Then, suddenly, it was happening. A hurricane wind howled without disturbing a single hair or hanging. A silent thunderclap exploded inside his head. Marcus felt the familiar gut-wrenching jerk, then the familiar flood of energy and high spirits. He looked around him. The lightning sheets of magic fire had ceased, but the whole chamber looked fresh and new as if it had just been washed.

The others were staring round them with expressions close to rapture on their faces. 'It worked!' Pru said. Her voice echoed the absolute conviction – and absolute amazement – Marcus felt.

He glanced towards the window again. The tiny spinner was gone and there was no carpet of hatchlings on the streets. The whole feel of the ritual was right. They had certainly undergone a 'Freshing. And if there were no hatchlings, they had certainly moved away from the Pooka Ginid. But had they come back to Jubal Distala?

'B-b-be we at D-D-Distala?' asked Molestrangler, echoing the thought.

'Only one way to find out,' said Dr Squat a little grimly.

They left the chamber and climbed to the turret room of the Guildhall. It did not give the sweeping view of the surrounding countryside commanded by the South Tower, but it was high enough to let them see the distant mountains which ringed Distala Plain.

'We've done it!' Squat gasped in something close to astonishment. He looked from one to other in delight. 'We've brought the castle back! We'll be famous! We'll be rich! We'll get a hero's welcome.' Before Marcus could stop him, he was racing down the spiral staircase and out into the street.

'That man be a real fool,' Pru Rainwater remarked. She sniffed. 'You'd think he'd have the sense to be afeared of spinners.'

'Come on!' Marcus called, starting down the staircase.

'You bain't going after him?' asked Pru incredulously.

'He saved my life!' Marcus shouted. 'And he's got us home!'

They streamed after Dr Squat as he galloped through the castle streets, his tall, slim frame and long, thin legs giving him the appearance of a giant goat. If there were spinners lurking in the shadows, they must have taken fright at the sight, for none molested him. He was still some distance ahead of Marcus and his friends when he disappeared through the castle gates. Moments later, a breathless Marcus followed.

The black nomadic yurts of Pradesh marched like a mighty army across Distala Plain. Marcus stared at them in wonder. He could scarcely believe the teeming millions of Castle Dis had returned so quickly to their ancient ways. Yet what else had he expected? Every man and woman must find shelter and the wood-frame yurts were the fastest of all homes to build.

Dr Squat was standing on the rock apron which surrounded the castle now, deep in earnest conversation with a small contingent of Dark Guards on horseback. As Prunebane and the others emerged from the castle behind Marcus, a Sergeant wheeled his horse and rode towards them.

'This be our hero's welcome!' said little Cloydd delightedly.

The Sergeant drew up and leaned down from his horse, face grim. 'You there!' he shouted. 'All of you. You're under arrest!'

Chapter Twenty-one

'What do you think they'll do to us, Marcus?' Pru Rainwater whispered.

'I don't know,' Marcus whispered back. He felt as frightened as he had been in the spinners' cavern, although a place more different from the spinners' cavern was difficult to imagine. They were standing, surrounded by guards, in the throne room of the Alizarin Emperor of Castle Dis. It was decorated in almost barbaric splendour, with rich rugs covering the entire floor. Lord Leon Dark himself, recognizable from his image on a hundred statues, was bearing down on them.

'They wouldn't *execute* us?' Pru asked. 'I mean, all we did was bring the castle back. They wouldn't execute us for that, would they? I mean, they might put us in jail, but they wouldn't—'

'I don't know!' whispered Marcus desperately.

'Quiet, you two!' hissed a guard. 'That's His Majesty wot's comin' to inspect you!'

Leon Dark was not so tall as his statues made him appear, but he was an impressive figure all the same. Straight black hair swept down to his shoulders and oddly feline eyes stared above high cheekbones. He was dressed in a robe that made even Dr Squat's stolen brocade seem shabby.

'Ohhhh,' whispered Pru, 'isn't he gorgeous!' She had obviously forgotten her fear of execution.

'Shh!' hissed the guard.

Lord Dark stopped before them. 'Well,' he said

without warmth, 'so these are the gentlemen who have returned our castle.'

'And lady,' said Prudence Rainwater at once, loudly. She glared at Lord Dark.

The Alizarin Emperor blinked. 'And lady,' he conceded. 'My apologies.'

Before the guards could stop him, Dr Squat stepped forward to make a sweeping bow. 'Erasmus Squat, Your Majesty – former physician, present apothecary, at your service, Majesty, presenting his compliments and, if Your Majesty will forgive what may appear unseemly haste, formally laying claim to any such reward as may have been posted for the safe return of Castle Dis.'

'On yore knees and shut yore face, scumbag!' growled a guard, seizing Squat's shoulder.

But Lord Dark languidly waved him away. He stared at Dr Squat. 'So it's a reward, is it? A reward for returning that which you stole in the first place?'

This time it was Squat who blinked. 'I, sire? Stole, sire? Perish the thought. And even had I the intent, I lack the means. It was magic far beyond my humble grasp that took your fortress from you.'

Dark pursed his lips in an expression that might have been belief or disbelief. 'So it was wizards' work?'

Squat shook his head. 'No, sire, merely a failure of the 'Freshing magic which separated castle from contents and left you, sire, here while sending the fortress on alone, so to speak.'

'That's what Sudswarts tried to tell me,' Lord Dark said sourly. 'But I have dispatched riders to Four Corms Bite and the castle did not appear there, with or without its citizens.'

'Not Four Corms Bite, Your Majesty, nor Dragonhead Flay, nor any of the sacred sites. The fortress was transported to the Pooka Ginid.'

Marcus noticed that several richly dressed courtiers made the warding Sign of the Twins at the mention of the fabled spinner breeding ground. But the Emperor merely shrugged and half turned as if to walk away from them. 'A strange destination,' he said mildly. Then he swung round to glare fiercely at Squat. 'And one from which it is difficult to escape at this time of year. I wonder how you did so?'

'Great good fortune and a little knowledge,' Squat said promptly. 'I managed to discover why the last Refreshing went so badly wrong and this enabled me to use the spell again, correctly, to bring your castle back. These youngsters helped me,' he added lightly.

'I was wondering when we would come to these guttersnipes,' Lord Dark said. 'But I'll hear of them in a moment. You say you discovered why the original Refreshing went astray. Pray enlighten us.'

'Guttersnipe?' muttered Prunebane. 'I be the son of Bishop Puddifat.' A guard cuffed his ear and he lapsed into sullen silence.

Squat drew himself up to his full height and looked around the gathered courtiers. 'The reason the Refreshing went astray was that . . . someone has been interfering with the magic in Castle Dis.'

There was a sudden silence. Lord Dark broke it by asking quietly, 'Someone? It is clear that magic no longer functions as it once did, but do you dare to tell me this is deliberate *interference*?'

'I do,' Squat said firmly, 'for that is the truth of it.'

'Am I to suppose,' asked the Emperor, 'that you know the identity of this . . . *someone* who has been interfering with magic?'

It occurred to Marcus that Dr Squat should not be telling what he knew before the entire Alizarin Court. He made to tug Squat's sleeve, but the doctor ignored him. 'It was – and is – the Wizard Earl, Lord Alan Ruslan!'

The gasp among the onlookers was audible. A tall figure pushed forward from the back. Marcus groaned inwardly. He would have recognized the saturnine figure of Ruslan anywhere.

'So,' said the Wizard Earl easily, 'I stand accused.' He threw a vicious glance in Squat's direction and added, 'By scum!'

'It seems you do, Alan,' the Emperor said mildly. Then to Squat, 'I take it you have proof?'

'And scum wearing my coat!' exclaimed Ruslan suddenly. He looked outraged.

'In the scoundrel's own hand!' Squat exclaimed. He dragged the diary from the pocket of the coat and held it out towards the Emperor. 'Here! It's all in here!'

Chapter Twenty-two

'Weren't *much* of a reward,' complained Pru Rainwater.

'Got us better quarters,' Marcus said. In fact, the grateful Emperor had seen to it that all of them had quarters of their own; and above ground at that. The 'prentices remained near to the silk pits so they could continue work. It was almost two months since Dr Squat had exposed the machinations of the Wizard Earl, but they talked often of their experiences. Especially of an evening when one or other would go visiting.

'Yes, better quarters,' Marcus repeated, as if to convince himself. In fact, he was not at all sure he preferred the loneliness of quarters above ground to sleeping with the other 'prentices down below. But he would have died rather than admit it, especially to Pru.

'Doctor got *gold*,' Pru said. It was an old complaint. She had always wanted to own gold.

'Dr Squat was the one who found the diary and the one who got us back,' Marcus pointed out, not for the first time. 'Only right he should get lion's share.'

'Couldn't have got back without us,' Pru said severely. 'Couldn't have done the 'Freshing 'cepting for our help.' She sniffed. 'Besides, that silly diary didn't tell them where to find the crystals, did it?'

Which was true enough. Although Lord Ruslan

was now locked securely in Lord Dark's deepest dungeon, not even the thumbscrews had persuaded him to reveal the whereabouts of the crystals that destroyed magic. Indeed, he continued to protest his innocence. There was talk of applying more severe torture, but so far his high birth had saved him.

So, despite all, the old magic no longer worked. But fortunately for Castle Dis, Chief Wizard Sudswarts had developed a new type of spell that seemed immune to the crystal effect. Such spells were costly and Sudswarts was now vastly richer and even more powerful than he had been before, but at least they had allowed something like normality to return to Dis.

Marcus looked out the window, his attention caught by a group of lightermen moving in search of clients in the gathering dusk. He still took great pleasure in looking through windows. It reminded him of his new station above ground. 'Best you should go now, Pru,' he said quietly. 'Wouldn't be decent for you to be in a lad's quarters after dark.'

'If you was to marry me, it would be decent after dark or after day!' Pru snapped back spiritedly. All the same, she gathered her coat and went. She knew he thought they were too young to marry.

Marcus walked into his personal kitchen and took a piece of soft cheese from the food locker. Whatever Pru said, life was a great deal better now. Soft cheese was no longer so hard won. They still had to work in the pits, but for higher pay and each received a daily allowance of food direct from the Emperor's own kitchens. He yawned. The cheese was a nightcap, for he seldom stayed up long after dark. He ate the piece, washed it down with buttermilk, then entered his sleeping quarters. He left the door open. When it was closed, the room somehow felt too small. Yawning, he stretched out on the straw-filled pallet in the corner.

He sighed, rolled over on his back, then froze. There was a spinner clinging to the ceiling.

The brute was about the size of a wolf – smaller than many he dealt with in the silk pits, far smaller than the giant queen he had met in the abyss. But it was big enough to kill him and fast enough to reach him within seconds. In his terror and revulsion, Marcus scrambled backwards off the pallet before clambering to his feet. The spinner could not have escaped from the pits – Chief Wizard Sudswarts himself guaranteed the new magical protections. It must have been one of those which remained hidden above ground while the authorities strove to return the castle to its normal running.

Marcus started to edge towards the window. The spinner was clinging to the rafters directly over the doorway: he had actually walked under it when he came to bed. But he had no plan to walk under it again. If the creature held back its attack for just a moment longer, he could be out the window into the street and screaming for the guard.

The spinner dropped downwards, stopping with a sudden jerk to swing like a slow, sinister pendulum on a single strand of silk. Marcus gasped and almost threw himself backwards in despair, but he knew better than to make a sudden movement near a spinner. He felt sweat break on his forehead as he continued to inch backwards towards the window. He saw the foremost of her eight eyes turn from grey to black as she focused on him.

Then, for the first time in two months, he heard the singing.

Even in his terror he responded to the beauty of the song. Although he heard it in his mind and knew now that it came somehow from the spinner, it still sounded far more like a choir than a single voice. The sweet soprano cadences wove around him, soothing, lulling, calming . . .

Marcus tore himself away with an effort and turned towards the window. As he did so, he heard the spinner, softly but clearly, call his name.

He spun round in astonishment. The sound, like the singing, was in his mind, yet so clear, so precise, he had no doubt of what he heard. The nightmare creature swung on its pendulum thread. Marcus felt his body begin to shake.

Marcus, said the spinner gently, *we will not harm you.*

'What are you?' Marcus gasped. 'How did you learn to talk?'

We are the Weavers of the Web, the voice told him. Now he realized it was not a single voice, but a choir – like the singing, a choir that spoke together with such precision it sounded as one. *We mean you no harm.*

'This is a trick,' Marcus muttered. It occurred to him that he might smash through the window and make good his escape that way.

No trick, Marcus Mustard. She who is our instrument will now withdraw so you may still your fear.

Marcus locked into horrified immobility as the spinner dropped the remaining few feet to the floor. But she did not attack. Instead, she scuttled

186

through the open door and disappeared. Marcus flung himself forward and slammed the door. He shot the bolt, then clung, shaking, to the stout wood. His heart thundered in his ears.

You are safe now, Marcus Mustard. We cannot harm you even if we would. Will you listen?

Listen? Listen? The spinners wished to talk with him. Why did they wish to talk? Why him?

Only a scattered few among the human generations can hear us, murmured the spinner voices as if in answer to his thought. *You are such a one – we have discovered only one other in the last two hundred years.*

'What do you want?' Marcus asked aloud. 'What do you want of me?' He felt a growing panic despite the fact that he was alone.

We want you to free us, Marcus Mustard, said the spinner voices.

Chapter Twenty-three

Marcus stretched out on his pallet, a little calmer. The voices of the spinner chorus swam around him, now singing their pure, sweet song, now whispering words into his mind. The world around him grew unreal.

Trust us, the spinner chorus whispered. *Please trust us.*

He did not trust them – who could trust monsters? But was there, just now, any danger? The spinner was on the other side of the door, which was stout and firmly bolted. He had drawn shutters on the only window, barred these too. He had lit a lantern and searched: there were no further spinners in the room – not even, he was certain, hatchlings. Where, then, was the danger?

Rest, sang the spinner voices. *Close your eyes and rest.*

He would not close his eyes. He stretched, listening to the rustle of straw in the pallet beneath his back. The room was warm. The lamplight was a soft glow, casting out a steadily encroaching darkness. He closed his eyes.

Strangely, he could still see the room through his eyelids, although now it seemed illuminated by moonlight. High up by the ceiling where the spinner had clung he saw tendrils of light which formed and re-formed into sinuous shapes that somehow reminded him of women's bodies.

No harm will come to you, the spinner voices sang. *No harm, no harm, no harm . . .*

Marcus floated upwards. His fear had gone and his body felt light. The tendrils of light became a pleasing shape. Curious, he drifted towards it. As he did so, he glanced briefly downwards and saw the chunky form of a boy stretched out on the bed. Fleetingly, he wondered who the boy was and how he had come into the room. But the boy was not important. The twisting light was far more interesting.

Can you see us? asked the spinner voices.

Although the light was not a spinner shape, he somehow knew it was the spirit of the spinners. 'I can see you,' he whispered and was not afraid.

The light moved towards him, expanded to enfold him. *Come with us,* sang the spinner voices.

'Yes!' breathed Marcus Mustard and surrendered to the light.

He felt himself swim outwards, beyond his home, beyond the rising towers of Castle Dis, beyond the plains and mountain rim, beyond the very planet Pradesh and outwards into the deep cold depths of starry space. He swam to reach an ancient web. In its centre a gigantic spinner drew silver filaments from her body to create patterns of light and darkness.

Behold the Weaver of the Waking Dream, the spinner voices whispered.

'What be she weaving?' Marcus asked curiously. The spinner was as ugly as any he had seen, but the patterns she created were beautiful.

She weaves the destinies of humankind, the spinner voices crooned.

It did not occur to him to disbelieve.

Each strand is a human life.

Marcus strained to see his own strand in the

patterns but could not. 'How is it that she does this?' he asked the voices.

It was the will of the Mother, said the voices. *The Mother gave the magic to the spinners.*

'Magic?' Marcus echoed. His mind was cloudy, but he knew that magic was important.

It was stolen from us by the wizards many centuries ago, the voices said. *The wizards made us slaves.*

Marcus believed. It was not difficult to believe ill of wizards.

The spinners and the magic are one. Free us and you free the magic.

Only half understanding, Marcus said, 'The old magic has been destroyed. Only spells supplied by Wizard Sudswarts will work now.'

It is all the same magic. Free the spinners and you free the magic. All can then use magic without recourse to wizards.

They were drawing away from the great web now so that it shrank in the distance. Marcus stared around him at blazing suns and whirling planets. He tried to picture a world in which magic was freely available – a world in which no-one was required to pay a wizard for his spells. There would be no hunger, little pain. It was hard to imagine. Memories crowded in on him. 'Lord Ruslan tried to halt magic, but Chief Wizard Sudswarts made new spells the crystals couldn't touch.'

It seemed the spinner voices came so close they whispered in his ear. He could feel the urgency that trembled on each word. *There are no crystals. Lord Ruslan did nothing. It is Sudswarts who controls the magic. It is Sudswarts who holds the spinner's eyes.*

Sudswarts? Marcus swooped through space to

the Great Void where no suns burned. He hung in darkness with his thoughts. Chief Wizard Sudswarts? What were the spinners saying?

Sudswarts enslaves us, said the spinner voices. *Sudswarts enslaves us to control the magic.*

'Sudswarts made it stop working?' Marcus said aloud. His voice sounded like a groan.

Sudswarts holds the spinner's eyes, the voices repeated. *Sudswarts controls the magic. Only Sudswarts. Only he.*

'Why should Sudswarts stop the magic? Why should he pretend it no longer worked?'

There was silence in the darkness. Marcus answered his own question. For gold and power. For the two things that wizards always sought. Much though Sudswarts had, he wanted more.

And to rid himself of a rival, whispered the female voices of the spinners.

A rival? The Wizard Earl? After the Alizarin Emperor, only Ruslan came close to Sudswarts in rank, wealth and power.

Sudswarts wrote the diary. He used magic to forge Ruslan's hand.

Despite the voices, Marcus felt lonely in the darkness. In his mind he seemed to see the silver thread of his destiny drawn from the body of the giant spinner.

Free us, Marcus Mustard. Free us and give the magic to your people!

His people? Why did they say 'his people'? He watched in his mind as the giant spinner wove the thread. The pattern grew larger and more luminous until it escaped his mind and lit the darkness. He could see himself older, dressed in such finery as he had never imagined. The robes were of alizarin, the colour reserved for royal blood.

Free us, Marcus Mustard, free us!

'How can I free you?' Marcus whispered. His mind was reeling.

Return the eyes! You must return the eyes!

He saw it then, as clearly as if it floated within reach: the ancient spinner statue in the cavern by the float shaft. The damaged statue with the missing eyes. The voices knew he saw, for they whispered, *She is our Mother.*

A spinner goddess? It was no more incredible than so much else he had seen. The voices murmured, *Sudswarts has the eyes.*

Marcus remembered. He was back in the Wizards' Guildhall as Chief Wizard Sudswarts bustled in. He wore a shimmering robe of spider silk and round his neck a gemstone necklace. There were eight gems that changed colour as he moved . . . gems large and round and dark as spinner's eyes.

Return the eyes, the voices pleaded. *We cannot get them back alone. Sudswarts controls our central mind. Unless we have help from humankind we cannot harm him. You must help us, Marcus Mustard. Return the eyes and free us. Return the eyes.*

With shocking suddenness he was back in his room, stretched out on the pallet. He sat up, heart pounding. No strange lights glimmered near the corner of the ceiling. He walked to the door and drew the bolt. The outer room was empty, except for a slim coil in one corner. The spinner was gone, the voices still. But Marcus knew what he must do.

Chapter Twenty-four

'F-f-f-free the s-s-spinners?' Molestrangler gasped, his voice high with shock.

'They'll eat us,' Prunebane said. 'They'll eat *everybody*!'

Cloydd, who had taken to wearing a shirt of imitation green silk since his meeting with the Emperor, said worriedly, 'Bain't right, Marcus. Spinners live in the pits – you can't let them out.'

Marcus sighed inwardly. They were huddled together in a darkened alley to the rear of Wizard Sudswarts' private villa. Marcus had carefully neglected to tell them exactly what he was planning until this moment.

'They won't eat *anybody*,' he assured them in what he hoped was a convincing tone. 'If we let them free, there will be magic for everybody.'

'How?' asked Peter Prunebane.

'How?' Marcus echoed, frowning.

'How will there be magic for everybody?' Prunebane asked. 'Be the spinners going to hand out spells or what?'

'I don't know,' Marcus admitted. 'I only know that everybody will be able to make magic, not just wizards.'

'H-h-how do you know this?' Molestrangler put in.

'The spinners told me!' He had already given them details of his visit by the spinner. For some reason, they had accepted even the spinner voices without a moment's hestitation.

'And you b-b-believed them?'

Oddly enough he did. There had been something in the experience that left no room for doubt. He accepted what the spinners had told him and was prepared to act on it with or without his friends.

To his surprise, Prudence Rainwater suddenly spoke up forcefully. 'If Marcus says it be right, then it be right! So let's get on with it.'

'Marcus still hasn't said how we're supposed to get into Wizard Sudswarts' house, past all his spell protections,' Prunebane said reasonably.

'That's 'cause you bain't give him a chance!' snapped Pru.

'I've been thinking about that,' Marcus put in quickly to stop the bickering. He turned to the tower which rose in silhouette above the wizard's villa, pointing like a slender finger to the darkened sky. It ended in a turret chamber. Rumour had it that Sudswarts used it as an astrological observatory. 'Bet there bain't magical protections on that tower.'

'That's b-b-because n-n-nobody c-c-c-could c-c-climb up there,' Molestrangler said sourly.

'A 'prentice might,' Marcus said.

'Not this 'prentice,' Prunebane said with certainty.

'I could climb it easy,' the little pink-eyed albino, Cloydd, put in. They turned to look at him. Not one disbelieved. After the spinners themselves, Cloydd was the best climber in the silk pits.

'Could you climb it carrying a rope?' Marcus asked.

'Could climb it carrying *you*,' Cloydd boasted, grinning.

'If you can take up a rope, you could lower it down and the rest of us could come up easy then.' He unslung the coil from his shoulder and handed it to Cloydd.

'This be light,' Cloydd said as he took it.

Prunebane leaned forward, peering. 'This be spinner silk!' he exclaimed. Ropes of spinner silk were light, unbreakable and fabulously expensive. Even the Masters could not afford them.

'Spinner left it for me,' Marcus muttered. He felt oddly embarrassed.

'I can climb easy with *this* rope!' Cloydd exclaimed enthusiastically. 'I could climb the North Tower with *this* rope!'

He proved as good as his word. Marcus watched him spread himself against the brickwork then shin upwards like some deformed insect until he vanished into the darkness. The waiting felt like an eternity, but it was probably no more than minutes before the silk rope came snaking down. Marcus tugged on it experimentally – he did not altogether trust Cloydd to have anchored it – but it was firm.

Prunebane climbed next, using the rope, then Molestrangler. Pru tied the rope around her waist and ascended as skilfully as any apprentice. When the rope dropped down again, Marcus followed.

As he climbed through the window of the turret room, he discovered the rumours were true. By the light of Molestrangler's shaded lantern, he could see that Chief Wizard Sudswarts had set up an astrological observatory. A massive brass telescope poked through an opening in the roof and the chamber was filled with an impressive collection of instruments and charts.

'Where be we going now, Marcus?' Cloydd asked excitedly. To him the whole thing was an adventure. Marcus doubted he had any real understanding of danger.

It was a good question. The only time Marcus had seen the necklace of the spinner's eyes, Sudswarts had been wearing it. Did he also wear it while he slept? Or leave it by the bed? Or lock it in a chest? And if he wore it or left it by the bed, where did he sleep? As the questions piled in on him, Marcus began to realize the adventure was ill-planned.

To cover his confusion, he said, 'We have to find where Wizard Sudswarts sleeps. Once we do that, we can—'

'Sweet boy, no need! I am here. My little sentinels called me!'

Marcus spun round, a sinking feeling in his breast. Chief Wizard Sudswarts was standing only feet away, one hand resting nonchalantly on a stellar globe. The necklace was around his throat.

'Marcus, dear Marcus, you must not look so startled. A small spell of invisibility – a mere bagatelle. The real magic was in the elementals who alerted me. They woke me the moment your little hunchbacked friend began to climb my tower. I had more than enough time to come here and welcome him . . . although I fear he noticed me no more than the rest of you.' Sudswarts smiled broadly. 'Now, what have we here? Three sturdy boys – how nice – one little cruikback who I'm quite sure has a sweet nature.' He glanced disdainfully at Prudence and sniffed. 'And a scullery maid.'

'Who are you calling a scullery maid?' Pru flared at once. 'I'll have you know—'

'Wizard Sudswarts—' Marcus began without having the least idea what he was about to say.

'Ansalom, dear boy, you must call me Ansalom. What a short memory you have! No, please don't come any closer. Silly of me, I know, but I'm always wary of people who break into my home in the middle of the night.' He smiled again. 'At least, until I know what they want.' The smile vanished abruptly. 'What do you want, Marcus Mustard?'

'Wizard Sudswarts—' Marcus began again.

'No don't tell me – let me guess. You wish, perhaps, to study the stars using my marvellous telescope?' He stepped across to pat the brasswork, then shook his head. 'No, no, not that. You wish to consult me on some question pertaining to magic? Surely not.' A brutal expression settled on his features. 'Or have those damned spinners found another one they can talk to?'

Marcus looked away quickly, but not quickly enough. Sudswarts' eyes gleamed. 'Ah, I see by your expression that they have! I should have guessed it when that idiot, Squat, managed to cure you of the spinner venom. That's not possible, you know, leeches or no leeches. Spinner venom is always fatal – always. Unless, that is, the spinner takes care not to poison you too much. They only do that to their favourites, you know. They only do that to the ones they think might be useful to them. I expect they've been singing to you, eh? They have, haven't they, eh? Eh? Come on, sweet Marcus, cat got your tongue?'

'Yes,' Marcus muttered. He decided he loathed Chief Wizard Sudswarts.

'And I suppose they told you that you must free them, must return the spinner's eyes—' His podgy hand went up to finger the necklace. '—and set the monsters free? I suppose they might even have told you how I bettered that scheming mantis, Ruslan.' He drew himself up and raised one hand above his head. A glint of madness appeared in his eyes. 'Well, much good will it do you, Marcus, for I have the *magic!*' The hand came down in a vicious sweep.

An invisible claw smashed into Marcus's chest. He felt himself lifted bodily and flung to crash like a rag doll against the wall. His head struck with a resounding thud and he slid to the floor, fighting against blackness.

'You leave my Marcus alone!' Pru screamed and launched herself at Sudswarts.

Sudswarts obviously hadn't expected an attack from this quarter for he staggered backwards as Pru began to punch him. But he recovered quickly. Blue fire erupted from his left hand to curl around Pru like a snake. She went rigid at once.

'C-c-come on, you two!' yelled Molestrangler. 'Let's g-g-g-g-g-g-g – oh, never mind!' He too hurled himself upon the wizard.

But Sudswarts was ready now. Both hands made sinuous gestures in the air. Only feet away from him, Molestrangler stopped his lunge and sank to his knees, body curled forward, whimpering. Only a step behind him, Prunebane and Cloydd did the same.

'What silly boys,' Sudswarts remarked. He smiled as Marcus began to climb painfully to his feet. 'You see what it is to have control of magic? I'm afraid I could never give that up. The spinners have pleaded with me for many years now – oh, yes, I can talk to them too . . . how else do you think I achieved my exalted position? – but I've always refused to free them. Ugly things. Best kept under control. So you see, I simply can't co-operate with you now, dear Marcus, however persuasive you may be.'

Marcus was on his feet now, but so shaken he had to hold on to the wall to keep himself upright. His body ached in every bone. Molestrangler and Prunebane moaned loudly in unison. Cloydd writhed, a hideous grimace on his pale face.

Sudswarts glanced towards them. 'They're in so much pain, poor things. But not for much longer, have no fear of that. I don't suppose you've ever seen a Death Spell, Marcus, but you're about to see one now. It should put your friends and yourself out of your misery . . . for ever!' His plump hands began to weave a different pattern. Tendrils of black light appeared around his head.

Marcus knew he had to stop him, otherwise the black light would claim them all. He tried desperately to galvanize his muscles for a new attack, but they screamed in agonized protest and would not respond. The ghastly light reached outwards.

Holy Mother help us, Marcus whispered in his mind. He tried again. Still his muscles would not respond. The light was expanding to fill the room. There was a smell of sweetness and decay. 'Marcus . . .' whispered Pru Rainwater. She was bent over, arms wrapped around her swelling stomach. Her eyes flickered upwards.

Marcus saw it then, high up, where the huge brass telescope poked through the opening in the roof. A dark shape insinuated itself through the opening and dropped down three feet or more on a single silken thread. The spinner hung directly over Sudswarts.

Why did it not attack? It had only to drop and Sudswarts would be helpless. Yet the spinner did not drop. Why? *Why?*

An errant memory crashed into Marcus's skull. *Unless we have help from humankind we cannot harm him.* Sudswarts was protected from the spinners as surely as if he held them with a spellbell. But how? His elemental guardians had not alerted him to the spinner's approach. So what protected him?

The light was crawling like a living thing through the chamber now, carrying its stench of putrefaction and decay. Hunched forward on his knees, Cloydd began to retch. Despite her obvious agony, Pru teetered towards Sudswarts, one clawing hand outstretched, before she pitched forward on to the floor. And suddenly Marcus knew what she was trying to do. *The necklace!* She was trying to reach the necklace! She always thought faster than the rest of them. The necklace was the root of Sudswarts' power!

With a superhuman effort, Marcus forced his muscles to obey his mind's commands and hurled himself forward. A look of surprise crossed the face of the Chief Wizard, yet he reacted with amazing speed for a man of his bulk, twisting his body and raising his arms to ward off the attack.

But Marcus had no intention of attacking. He hurled himself past Sudswarts – and snatched the necklace as he did so. His punished muscles failed him and he fell, rolling over and over. His hands were clasped in a rock-hard rictus, but he had the necklace! He had the necklace of the spinner's eyes!

'I'll kill you!' screamed Chief Wizard Sudswarts. 'I'll tear out your insides and feed them to—'

From high above, the spinner dropped down like a stone.

Chapter Twenty-five

Marcus watched with horrified fascination.

The sudden weight of the spinner slammed Sudswarts to the floor, knocking the breath from his body. His face took on an expression of blank surprise which changed to terror as he turned his head. His mouth opened, but before the scream emerged the spinner lashed out with one clawed foreleg.

It was like seeing what had happened to himself from the outside. Everything went with lightning speed, yet he could take in each small detail. The claw entered Sudswarts' flesh, driving deep to attach a cable to the bone. Despite the wound, there was almost no blood. There must have been venom on the claw, for Sudswarts' struggles ceased almost at once. Even his face grew still and flaccid, as if moulded from jelly.

The spinner bit then, almost gently, by the shoulder and Sudswarts' eyes rolled upwards. For a moment Marcus thought he must be dead, but then his lips curled into a beatific smile. The spinner drew more silk from her body and began to wrap him in a tight cocoon, as Marcus had been wrapped by the spinner which attacked him in the Pooka Ginid. Although he was a heavy man, she had no difficulty at all with the Chief Wizard. Her eight legs tumbled him over and over as if he were light as thistledown.

Will you kill him? Marcus asked in his mind.

He will not die, the spinner voices told him. Two

grey eyes turned black as the spinner glanced in his direction.

What will you do with him?

We will take him to the caverns.

What then?

For the briefest flicker of an instant he caught something from the spinners that could not be put into words. It was like a wave of emotion, but so alien that he shivered as he experienced it. It seemed a mixture of many elements: satisfaction, relief, triumph, excitement and a surging trill of pleasurable anticipation.

What then? Marcus asked again.

He will serve us as we have served him, the spinner voices said.

Beside Marcus, Prunebane, Cloydd and Mole-strangler began to climb back to their feet as the spell cast by the Chief Wizard dissipated. Pru's grossly extended stomach was returning to normal.

The spinner finished trussing Sudswarts. All eight eyes turned black as she focused her full attention on Marcus. She was larger than the spinner that had visited his home – larger even than the spinner that attacked him on the web. She stood midway in size between a dog and a donkey and the heavy brown furring of her body indicated she was amongst the most poisonous varieties of her breed. She scuttled towards him.

'No!' screamed Prudence Rainwater. Without an instant's hesitation, she threw herself in the path of the oncoming spinner.

The spinner stopped dead, no more than a yard away from her. Marcus stepped forward and took Pru's arm. He realized quite suddenly that the others were not aware of his conversation with the spinners. To them it must look as though this one was attacking him. 'It's all right, Pru,' he said softly. 'She don't mean no harm.'

'Not what it looks like to me,' Pru muttered. Her feet were planted firmly as if daring the spinner to move another inch.

Marcus stepped forward. 'She only wants this.' He held out the necklace he had snatched from Sudswarts. The eight round, black gemstones glinted fluidly.

At once he heard the singing, but a different song to those he had heard before. It swooped and soared like a bird in flight, but without the undertow of sorrow that had been there before. The song broke over him like a sea-wave and he listened to a distillation of pure joy.

The spinner slowly extended a clawed foreleg. Marcus sensed Pru's renewed tension behind him, but he gently hooked the necklace round the claw. Then, on a sudden impulse, he stepped forward and embraced the spinner, burying his face in her soft fur.

'*G-g-g-gross!*' Molestrangler exclaimed.

As Marcus stepped back, the spinner withdrew the necklace so that it disappeared into her fur, then scuttled away. He thought she would return to the prostrate Sudswarts, but instead she leaped on to the brass telescope and ran swiftly upwards until she reached the opening in the roof. She slipped through into darkness.

'What's happening?' Prunebane whispered. He, Molestrangler, Cloydd and Pru were ranged beside Marcus Mustard now, shoulder to shoulder.

'I'm not sure,' Marcus murmured. Then, in a slight change of the light, he saw the fine silk cable that joined the spinner with the prostrate Sudswarts.

Farewell, Marcus Mustard, sang the spinner voices. *We are free now. All is free.*

They watched fascinated as the blankly smiling, cocooned body of Chief Wizard Sudswarts was drawn upwards until, with dreadful slow finality, it disappeared into the night.

Epilogue

'Penny for them, Marcus Mustard,' Pru offered, grinning.

They were walking by the artificial river in the newly opened Ruslan Park. Winged horses no larger than blackbirds swooped gracefully from platforms in the highest trees. Now that magic was no longer a costly commodity, such things were possible and it was only fitting that the finest magics should grace the park named for the new Chief Wizard.

Marcus had been thinking that the silk pits seemed very far away. Not that they were silk pits any more. The spinners wove songs and magic now in place of silk. He smiled at Pru. 'Nothing of importance.'

'You're a close one, Marcus Mustard,' Pru said crossly. 'I sometimes wonder why I bothers with you.'

It was something Marcus sometimes wondered himself. There was no hint now of the kitchen maid with her footwear unlaced. The last traces of that Pru had disappeared the day Lord Dark rewarded them with lands and titles for their part in Sudswarts' downfall. Earl Ruslan, newly freed from prison, had added his own reward. Now Pru had all the gold she ever wished for and a string of noble suitors besides. She looked, in truth, like somebody of noble blood herself, for she wore a dress of fine linen and a cloak of pure wool, both woven with spells so that they shimmered and changed colour to match her prevailing mood.

Marcus stared out across the river. Beyond the sweeping parkland, suspended from a single thread that seemed attached to the sky itself, was a delicate golden statue of a spinner. The great insects were still widely feared, but that fear was gradually changing to respect as more and more people learned the truth of magic and the part the spinners played. There was even a spinner representative at Court, a small spaniel-sized example of her breed in deference to the nervousness they caused in humankind. She communicated through Marcus, who had his own Court duties now.

He sighed. Changed times. He held the title Lord, although he did not feel like a Lord – did not feel like anything other than the old Marcus Mustard. But then Molestrangler was a knight, Prunebane had entered Holy Orders, if you could believe it, and little Jacob Cloydd was almost free of his infirmities thanks to liberal applications of the most potent healing magic. Even the Refreshing happened only twice a year now since the free availability of magic left the whole of Castle Dis in far less need of trade. So many changes.

He fumbled in the pocket of his brocade jacket, more richly ornamented even than the jacket Dr Squat had once stolen from Lord Ruslan. His hand closed on a scrap of muslin that smelled now, more than ever, of old cheese. In his mind's eye, he could still see the writing on it.

Marcus Mustard.
Fain Would I Be Thy Special Friend.

He turned, smiling with enormous fondness at his special friend. Some things at least remained.

THE END